Published 2019 in the United States of America by Timberdoodle Press LLC.

Cover art courtesy depositphoto.com

Ebook ISBN #978-1-945856-62-4

Print ISBN #978-1-945856-61-7

Large Print ISBN #978-1-945856-83-9

TWISTED SISTER

CHARLEY MARSH

TIMBERDOODLE PRESS LLC

1

————

FAITH STRETCHED and curled back up inside her down sleeping bag. She had to pee and her toes were starting to get cold, but she didn't want to leave her warm cocoon. The snow beneath her body creaked as she shifted into a more comfortable position.

A dull ache thumped its way through her head as she lifted it and repositioned the lumpy pile of clothes that blocked the cold air waiting outside the bag's opening.

She never should have listened to her sister. Bridal shower or not, drinking champagne in the bitter cold was dangerous. Winter camping required intelligence and stamina. Alcohol inhibited both.

She scrunched her wool shirt into a tighter ball,

tucked its rough surface under her cheek, and drifted back to sleep until the urge to pee became too strong to ignore.

Faith opened her eyes and poked her head out of her bag. Her nose practically touched the tent sidewall. The small tent was a tight squeeze for two bodies and their gear, especially when both sisters stood nearly six feet tall in stocking feet.

The inside surface of the igloo tent was rimed with a light coat of white, prickly frost. She watched, fascinated, as the spikes of frost quivered and disintegrated under her warm breath.

The cold air from the tent wall wafted onto her face and cleared the fuzziness from her brain. She could feel the chill of the frozen snow under the tent floor seeping through her sleeping pad and bag.

Faith closed her eyes again and tried to ignore her full bladder. If Hope was still sleeping she didn't want to wake her. Hope was never pleasant when woken before she was ready to get up.

The sisters had set up camp very late last night. Faith had been exhausted after a full day's work followed by the long drive from Falmouth to the town of Greenville situated on the southern tip of Moosehead Lake.

Her sister Hope had let Faith drive from Falmouth to Greenville, then insisted that they head for the woods immediately even though Faith had wanted to spend the night in Greenville and leave for the woods in the morning.

After several long, dark hours on snowmobile the sisters had finally set up camp at the base of a small mountain. They shared a bottle of champagne to celebrate Faith's upcoming wedding. The long day and bubbly had finished Faith off. She couldn't remember crawling into her bag.

She couldn't ignore the urge to pee any longer. Hadn't one of their teachers—Mrs. Halstead probably, as she loved to lecture on the perils of ignoring common sense—once told the girls that they would get bladder infections if they tried to hold their urine for too long?

"Hope?" Faith called softly. No point in waking her sister if she still slept.

"Hope? You awake?"

Faith rolled onto her back and looked to her right. The spot that should have held Hope's sleeping bag was empty. She frowned at the blank space. Since when had Hope ever been awake and moving before her? Apparently that bottle of champagne had more kick than Faith had realized.

"Hope?" she called louder. Maybe Hope had taken the camp stove outside and had water boiling for tea.

The thought of drinking more fluid set Faith's teeth on edge. If she didn't pee right now she was going to burst. She pushed her wool pants down into the bag and struggled to pull them up over her long, underwear-clad legs.

Winter camping required multiple layers of clothing. Too many, Faith realized. She wasn't going to make it.

She unzipped her bag and grabbed her felt-lined boots. Pee first, dress after. She jammed her feet into the boots and crawled on her hands and knees to the tent door. Her knees left shallow, bowl-shaped depressions in snow under the tent floor.

She unzipped the screen door, then the solid door, and crawled onto the ground tarp that lined the narrow vestibule floor. Her bare hands sunk into snow.

The ground tarp was gone.

"Not funny, Hope!"

Faith had often been the brunt of her sister's cruelty growing up. It had been several years since Hope had pulled one of her tricks; long enough for Faith to begin to believe that maybe—maybe—her older sister had finally outgrown the need to harass her.

Faith grumbled a curse. Apparently she would always have to be on guard against Hope's unpleasant jokes. The inevitable confrontation would have to wait or she'd be wearing wet pants in frigid temps, never a good idea.

Faith rocked to her feet and crab-walked out of

the vestibule. She whipped down her pants and squatted in the snow, moaning with relief as she emptied her bladder.

It wasn't until she had pulled her pants back up and looked around the tent site that she realized Hope had gone.

Faith shivered and blinked against the bright snow. The sun was well up over the horizon—mid-morning, she guessed. A gust of wind tore through her inadequate clothing and she dove back into the tent to finish dressing.

She pulled on her red buffalo plaid wool shirt and struggled to button it with trembling fingers.

What kind of prank was Hope up to this time? Why had Hope left Faith here? This was more than a prank. Abandoning Faith in the winter woods of northern Maine could easily turn into a death sentence.

She added her bulky, navy wool fisherman's sweater, kicked off her boots, and pulled wind pants on over her thick, wool pants. While most modern campers went for the latest hi-tech fabrics like polypro, Faith preferred good old-fashioned wool.

She tried to avoid all clothing made from man-made fabrics, opting for natural fibers like silk and cotton instead. Wool was one of her favorites. It was not only a versatile natural fiber, it kept a person warm even when it got wet.

She had a feeling that would soon be important to her survival.

Faith knelt down and pulled her mittens, scarf, and balaclava from the toe of her sleeping bag. Stuffing them down there was the last thing she remembered doing from the previous night. That was before the bottle of champagne.

She pulled the light balaclava over her head and wrapped the scarf around her neck, then looked around the tent for her heavy winter parka. It was nowhere in sight.

A small frisson of fear prickled the back of Faith's neck as she flipped the empty sleeping bag aside to check underneath.

No parka. Her loving sister had stranded her in the north woods without adequate protection from the elements.

She set her mittens aside and considered her situation while she rolled up her sleeping bag and stuffed it into its stuff sack.

Hope was gone. She had taken Faith's snowmobile and its small pull-behind trailer with all their food and survival gear, including the snowshoes.

She'd left Faith with only the tent and her sleeping bag.

This explained why Hope had claimed her new snow machine was in the shop for repairs. It also explained why Hope had insisted they come on the planned bridal shower camping trip anyway.

Faith's hand shook as she wiped the tears from her cheeks. What a fool she had been. Would she never learn? She had wanted so desperately to believe that Hope had changed her ways that she had been thrilled when Hope suggested this trip in lieu of a regular bridal shower.

It would be great, Hope had told her. Just us sisters, the nearly identical Irish twins, born thirteen months apart—sisters who should have been closer and more alike—on a winter camping trip in the wilds of northern Maine to celebrate Faith's upcoming marriage and the completion of her latest novel.

Faith tossed the stuff sack out the tent door, pulled on her mittens, and crawled out after the bag.

A sharp wind whistled through the tree tops overhead. Invisible molecules of ice cut through her sweater and attacked every cell of exposed skin on her face.

The sunlight reflected off the snow, a white hinterland strewn with glittering jewels that blinded her with their dazzle and made her eyes tear. She crawled back into the tent and dug her tinted goggles out of the small side pocket, thankful that exhaustion had made her stuff them into the tent pocket last night instead of placing them in the snow machine's seat compartment like she usually did.

Faith exited the tent once more and turned a full circle, inspecting the surrounding landscape. Around her stood the sentinels of the northern mountains: slim, straight trunks of silver-gray aspen and white paper birch dotted with dark stands of evergreens.

She took a deep breath, drawing the crisp, icy air deep into her lungs. She had always loved winter camping—loved the bracing, pure cleanliness of the air and the sparkling snow, the utter stillness and quiet.

This was not a bridal shower. Nor had Hope's plan been spur of the moment. Faith could see that now. This was a well thought out act of pure malice, concocted in the mind of a sister so twisted with jealousy that she had no scruples about leaving Faith here to die.

Anger began to to seep in and push out the sadness Faith always felt whenever Hope betrayed her with yet another cruel trick. She squared her shoulders. She was not going to let Hope get away with it.

A snowmobile track marked the snow to one side of the tent. A single line that circled and rejoined itself before heading off into the distance until it disappeared from sight. Faith's snow machine, Faith's gear, all stolen by her not-so-loving sister.

She must have been dead to the world not to hear Hope leave.

Faith pulled off her mittens with a heavy sigh and bent to the task of taking down the tent. She had shelter and a warm sleeping bag; boots, but no snowshoes or cross-country skis. No food, no water, no way to melt snow.

She rolled the tent tightly and stuffed it into its carry sack along with the rainfly and poles, then struggled to her feet and pulled her mittens back over her stiff hands.

She also had no pack to carry the sleeping bag and tent in. She had no choice but to carry them—without protection from the elements she had no chance of survival. With them she had a slim chance of getting out of her predicament alive.

She eyed her sleeping pad. A self-inflating air pad, it had already puffed up in size even though she had closed the air valve when she emptied it. She needed the insulation from the cold snow, but she could only carry two items.

Faith knelt and dug a narrow trench in the snow and reluctantly buried the sleeping pad under the snow. At least burying the pad would prevent it from blowing around the woods. She couldn't bear to litter. She even stooped to pick up other people's trash when walking through her neighborhood.

When—*if*—she survived, she thought angrily, she

would never speak to Hope again. And she would draw up a new will. As her only living relative, Faith had left everything to her sister. Now she'd look for a charity to give it to instead.

If she survived.

She stomped down the snow over the pad, hefted a stuff sack under each arm and stepped onto the snowmobile track. Her boot promptly sank up to her left shin in the packed powder.

They had come at least fifty miles from where they had left Faith's truck and snowmobile trailer. The nearest small town was another forty miles beyond that.

Ninety miles. Ninety impossible miles through deep snow, one slow step at a time. For a moment the hopelessness of the task she faced overwhelmed her.

Faith took several deep breaths to calm her fear and stepped with her right foot. She pulled her left foot free and took another step, stretching her leg as far as it would go. Fewer steps would use up less of her energy, she reasoned.

She struggled forward, one slow step at a time. Pull a foot free, stretch, set it down, balance, repeat. Within twenty minutes she had pulled down her balaclava and unwound her scarf.

Beads of moisture rolled down her back and the fear-tainted, sour scent of her own sweat mixed with the wool's lanolin rose from her damp clothes.

The snowmobile track meandered over the wooded slope. Hope had driven Faith's machine last night, insisting that it was only fair since Faith had driven from Falmouth to the place where they left her truck.

Hope had followed the official snowmobile trail for the first hour, then veered away from it despite Faith's protests that it was safer to keep to the marked trail.

Of course Hope had left the marked trail, Faith thought bitterly. Her sister wouldn't want to risk another snowmobiler coming along and rescuing Faith. Her sister's actions were all so obvious now.

Faith followed the snowmobile track between a pair of large, old growth oak trees. Every thirty steps she stopped to catch her breath. Faith kept herself in good physical condition, but the effort required to move through deep snow was pushing her heart rate.

She leaned against one of the ancient oak trees, welcoming the irritation of the rough, gnarly bark against her bare cheek. She pressed her face against it, reminding herself that she was still alive, still not beaten by her sister and the beautiful winter wonderland that she loved.

A faint breeze wafted through the trees and carried the pleasant fragrance of balsam fir to her. The balsam scent reminded Faith of Christmas trees and loving, storybook families and renewed her determination to survive.

The low drone of a small, unseen plane flying overhead taunted her. It was the first civilized sound she'd heard since Hope had abandoned her.

Faith cried out and struggled to run into the open. If she could catch the pilot's attention he would send a search party for her. But the snow prevented her from moving fast enough and the engine's drone faded away before she could get out from under the trees.

She fought down the feeling of helplessness that threatened to overwhelm her and trudged, one step at a time, until the sun touched the mountaintops. She found a flat spot and set up the tent, then crawled inside her bag without removing her clothes and tried to ignore her complaining belly.

She could live without food. Water was a more pressing problem. She had scooped snow into her mouth regularly, but melting snow robbed her body of precious heat and energy.

The night was long and cold, so cold that she heard the occasional tree crack as it contracted. Without her air pad the cold seeped through the tent floor and into her sleeping bag. She removed only her boots and rolled herself into a tight ball in an attempt to conserve her body heat.

Outside the tent the wind picked up, rattling

bare branches overhead. It whistled down the mountainside and snapped the edges of the tent fly. Faith shivered and prayed the wind would die down before sunrise. She knew she would not survive another day of exposure to its icy bite.

2

FAITH'S already lagging spirits dropped even further when she crawled out of the tent the next morning and saw fresh snow. To make matters worse, the wind's velocity had increased overnight.

Tearing down the tent in the gusting wind proved to be impossible in her weakened state. Leaving it behind wasn't an option: the tent was her home, her only refuge from the weather.

She stared at the orange dome and tried to think. The relentless wind cut through her clothing, seeking to caress her skin with its icy fingers. She shivered and wished she had a cup of hot coffee.

After several minutes—her brain was getting so fuzzy—she removed her scarf, tied one end around her waist and the opposite end through one of the tent's stake loops.

Dragging the tent behind her slowed her already sloth-like pace, but she refused to cut it loose. The tent meant survival, and her mind had focused down on that single concept: to survive she needed the tent.

She must survive. She had a few words to say to Hope before she cut her sister from her life forever.

The new snow had obliterated the snowmobile track. Without a clear path back to civilization, Faith knew she would soon be hopelessly lost.

She needed to get out of the wind, she decided. At the very least, she could minimize the issues she had to deal with. She descended the hillside. Several times the tent snagged on trees and she was forced to turn back and work it free.

The hill's bottom spread into a wide, flat, open plain. Her spirits rose. She remembered crossing the plain last night on their way in to the camp site. Or was it the night before?

What did it matter? What did anything matter? Her life had become an endless series of steps through a white hell. Discouragement filled her. Tears rolled onto her goggles and froze there. She kept putting one foot in front of the other. Left. Right. Left. Right.

She knew that under the flat expanse of snow

lay a peat bog full of brown, tannic water. Water she couldn't access. Water she desperately needed to replace what her body lost as she continued to perspire despite the frigid temperature.

She fell to her knees and dug down into the snow until she reached the smooth ice surface. She tried to break the ice with her fist but it was much too thick. She gave up, scooped another mouthful of snow into her mouth and shivered as the cold hit her teeth.

A wind gust came barreling across the open bog, stirring up snow devils as it approached her. It cut through her layers of wet clothing and stung her skin with its icy knives. The tent danced crazily to her left, jerked to a stop when it reached the end of its tether, and rolled to her right, almost pulling Faith over.

In the wind the tent acted like a drag, like the chutes employed to slow down dragsters on the race track. It slowed her pace even further but she refused to leave it behind. The tent meant survival. She had to survive. She couldn't let Hope win.

The tent meant survival. She couldn't let Hope win. The mantra repeated itself over and over. Faith clamped her chattering jaw tight, bent into the wind and struggled forward.

Step. Lift. Step. Balance. Lift. Step. Balance.

The distance between her steps became shorter and shorter as her thigh muscles wearied. She ignored the intense burn in her quads and forced her legs to lift her heavy boots again and again.

Lift. Step. Balance.

Another strong gust of wind whirled out of nowhere and knocked her sideways, burying her sleeping bag in the snow. She lay on top of the stuff sack, gasping, pulling the cold air into her straining lungs, while the tent danced around her as if possessed.

How far had she come? Ten miles? Three miles? Two? One? Only eighty-nine to go.

"Aidy-nine bottles of beer on the shelf, aidy-nine bottles of beer. Take one down and pash it around, aidy-eight boddles of beer."

Faith whispered the old drinking song she had learned as a teen. She was slurring, she noticed. That wasn't good.

A cold beer would taste so good right now. Her tongue felt swollen and was beginning to cleave to the roof of her mouth. The relentless cold continued to seep through her layers of clothing. She pulled off her mitten and scooped more snow into her mouth, waited for it to melt.

She struggled to her knees and then to her feet. She forgot the sleeping bag buried in the snow.

She had to keep moving. She had to see Hope.

Step. Gather her energy. Step.

Her eyes teared from the hours spent staring at the glaring snow. Her tears left white salt tracks on the goggles and froze into a crust of ice on the bottom rim but she had no way to clean them. Her lips felt rough and cracked.

Her legs began to tremble with fatigue. Her empty stomach demanded fuel to keep her body working.

Faith trudged on. Her world narrowed to one word.

Step. Step. If she stopped she would die.

She had long ago given up trying to scoop out the snow that filled her boots and her feet were numb and ached at the same time.

Step.

No matter how hard she struggled, Faith couldn't pull her right leg out of the snow to take another step. She threw herself forward and tried to crawl. Her arms sunk in the snow up to her shoulders.

She tried to roll free but couldn't summon the strength. She wept and howled with anger and frustration.

She knew the truth now. She would not make it out of the north woods alive. She was going to die here and some wild animal would find her and feast upon her flesh.

If not eaten, her body would sink into the bog once the ice melted, and Faith Donahue, successful writer and twenty-seven year old virgin, would disappear from the face of the earth.

Only Richard, her fiancé, would notice, because she had no friends. Hope had driven them all away. Hope always drove anyone that Faith cared about away, male or female.

It had been laughably easy for Hope to lie to anyone who tried to befriend Faith. Easy for her sister to make Faith out to be a stand-offish snob who felt others were beneath her notice, when in truth Faith was painfully shy.

Only Richard seemed immune to Hope's games. For some strange reason, Hope had accepted Richard in Faith's life.

Faith rolled onto her back. The wind ceased to torment her down here, snuggled into the soft snow. She sighed. It felt so good to rest. The shivering had stopped and she felt surprisingly comfortable.

She thought about the beautiful dress she had bought for the simple wedding ceremony that was scheduled to take place next Saturday. A simple deep bronze silk sheath. The saleswoman had assured her that it set off her dark red hair and pale skin. It was the nicest dress Faith had ever owned.

Now she'd never get to see Richard's face when he saw her in it. Never get to experience what a man's hands and mouth felt like on her body. She had been a fool to wait, but Richard had never pushed her for sex. He had been a perfect gentleman, patient and willing to wait until their wedding night.

Hope would win the war she had been waging ever since they could both talk. Faith's deep desire to finally have a normal relationship with her twisted sister had finally done her in.

She closed her eyes and rested in the bright sun.

3

———

WADE ELLIOT GRUNTED with effort as he wrestled the large section of pine log onto his sled. He lashed it to the sled's metal frame so it wouldn't roll off and connected the sled's lines to his body harness.

He had been working on a design for this log ever since he had pulled it from the bog last summer, and now he felt ready to begin his most ambitious project yet.

Wade pulled his dark sunglasses from his down vest pocket and put them on. He had learned the hard way that the glare of the sun off the snow that covered the bog could cause snow blindness in a very short space of time. It was an experience he did not wish to repeat.

He checked the bindings on his snowshoes and

started through the alder grove that grew in the swampy south end of the bog. He had left the pine log to dry on a hummock of land that rose above the swamp, planning to retrieve it once the bog had frozen.

The log had proven to be too large and heavy to transport by his canoe during the summer. He expected to need two days to drag it up the length of the bog to where his cabin lay at the opposite end. He would haul it halfway home today, return to his cabin for the night, and finish the task tomorrow when he was fresh.

There was no rush after all. Ever since leaving the Boston PD Wade did things on his own time frame. He ate when he was hungry, slept when he felt tired, wandered through the woods when he felt restless or his demons were hounding him.

It had taken nearly two years of solitude, but he felt brief moments of peace now. Moments when memories of his last days as a homicide detective were not forefront in his mind.

Wade leaned forward and felt the harness dig into his broad shoulders as he used his long, powerful legs to propel the sled forward. He soon pulled clear of the alder patch and headed up the east side of the bog.

Movement in the corner of his eye caught his attention and he stopped to check it out. The

Maine woods were full of wildlife and he always made time to observe whatever crossed his path.

Last week he had watched a lynx that had wandered near his cabin stalk and catch a rabbit. He had felt bad for the rabbit, but rabbits were prolific and plentiful, put upon the earth to feed the larger predators such as the much rarer lynx, owls, coyotes and foxes. Prey and predator were part of the order of life.

Except when it came to humans. Humans who preyed upon other humans were monsters. Wade had devoted his professional life to hunting the human monsters. Until they had turned on him and he had flamed out.

Wade slid the day pack off his shoulder and pulled out a pair of compact binoculars. He fit the rubber eyecups to his sunglasses and scanned the west side of the bog.

A patch of orange jumped back and forth on the snow.

A weather balloon? No, they were usually made from silver mylar. He watched the object for a few moments. It appeared to be snagged on something that looked like a log or a small missile. A parachute perhaps?

Should he take the time to stop and check it out? The unidentified object was out of his way. The bog's eastern shore was the direct path to his cabin. It was a good mile to where the object bounced around.

Too far. What if the object broke loose and blew away before he reached it? He would have wasted all that time and energy for nothing.

He looked down at the log on the sled. The tannins from the bog had seeped into the pine's cells, rendering it a soft honey brown and preserving the wood. His fingers twitched, eager to start the new project.

On the other hand, the log had lain in the bog for decades. What was one more day?

"Aw, hell." Wade released the harness clasp and headed up and across the bog on a long diagonal. As he neared the foreign object the hairs on the back of his neck lifted. He hated that feeling—it usually meant that something was very wrong.

Soon he could clearly make out the classic dome shape of a small tent. The tent appeared to be snagged on a long log. A blue log.

Wade grabbed hold of the fluttering tent and quickly released one end of the poles. It collapsed on the snow like an orange shroud. He stepped around the tent and approached the still body.

It lay on its back, arms spread-eagled as if it had been caught in the act of making snow angels. There was no movement, no sign of life.

"Stupid bastard," Wade said as he knelt beside the body. He had responded to a call once that involved an alcoholic who had passed out in a snowbank and never woke up. He'd never forget the frost on the man's eyelashes.

He saw the hole dug down to the ice. Hypothermia was not only deadly, it sometimes induced strange behavior.

Wade had looked into the condition on the off-chance that he might be faced with another case one day. People who suffered from hypothermia often tried to burrow, the same way hibernating animals burrowed. Sometimes when they passed the shivering stage they felt warm, and removed clothing.

He wondered if this bloke had removed his parka and lost it. At least he'd had the sense to hang onto his tent. Not enough sense to wrap it around himself though to cut the wind.

Wade knelt down beside the body and pulled off the body's goggles, slipping them into his pocket. He pulled up the balaclava. A thick mass of long curly hair tumbled against the snow. He rocked back on his heels and stared at the mahogany colored locks in disbelief.

"Well, hell."

What was a woman doing alone in the north woods of Maine in the dead of winter? He recalled the snowmobile engine he had heard two nights ago. Had she broken down and tried to walk out of here to get help?

Wade pulled the balaclava back down over her face. He was getting to his feet when the woman's eyes fluttered briefly, startling him. He stared down at her in disbelief. Had he imagined the movement or was she alive?

Wade whirled away and headed back to his sled as fast as he could. Once there he untied the log and rolled it off, reattached the sled to his harness, and made his way back to the frozen woman.

He pulled the sled alongside the woman's body and unclipped the harness, then untied the scarf from her waist. He pulled one of the tent poles free, rammed it deep into the snow, and slid a stake loop over it.

That should keep her tent here until he could come back and get it. For some reason, perhaps because the woman had worked so hard to hang onto her tent, he wanted to be able to return it to her.

If she survived.

Now for the tricky part. Hypothermia victims were very fragile. Wade knew that excessive or jarring movement could trigger cardiac arrest. He was afraid that even the act of lifting her onto the sled could be dangerous.

He considered the problem for a minute, then moved the sled aside and dug a trench under it and slid the sled into the trench. He picked up the woman's boots and swung her legs down onto the sled, then slowly lifted her torso and gently placed it on the sled.

He saw no sign of life from the woman while he did this. Wade had no idea if she had already expired and he didn't want to waste precious time searching for a pulse. One way or another, he couldn't leave the body here for the scavengers.

He reattached the sled's harness and strained forward. The loaded sled hesitated, then popped out of the shallow trench, sending him sprawling to his hands and knees.

He cursed and struggled to his feet, lifted the tips of his snowshoes out of the snow, and began the trek back to his cabin. Along the way he tried to recall everything he had read about treating hypothermia.

Even if he couldn't find a pulse when he got the woman into the cabin, it was important to proceed as if she was alive until he knew for certain that she was not.

The cold could have slowed down her blood flow to the point where he wouldn't be able to feel her pulse. Besides, he was no doctor—better to err on the side of assuming she lived.

She was obviously a fighter. She had tried to hike out of the north woods in the dead of winter with no parka and no snowshoes. Either a fighter or a fool. He hoped she lived so he would learn the answer.

Despite the cold wind, Wade was sweating lightly when he reached the rustic log cabin set partway up Mulligan's Mountain. He turned the sled perpendicular to the hillside so it wouldn't slide back down before releasing the harness. He quickly bent down, removed his snowshoes, and jammed them into the snowbank beside the steps.

The woman hadn't moved or made a sound during the trek to the cabin, although to be fair, all he could see were her closed eyes. He took the wide wooden steps up to his front porch two at a time and flung open the cabin's heavy front door.

The fire in the wood stove had died down and the air in the cabin had cooled, but it felt balmy compared to the outside temperature.

He needed a way to get the woman inside. If he tried to carry her he would jolt her and possibly kill her. The best way to move her would be to leave her in the sled and bring the whole thing inside.

Wade grabbed the blue and white star quilt his sister had made him for Christmas four years ago along with a roll of duct tape, then ran back out of the cabin. He looked at the quilt. Would the duct tape ruin it?

Swearing, he ran back inside, flung the quilt into a chair and grabbed a woolen blanket off the bed. He tucked the blanket around the woman's body and secured her to the sled with several wraps of tape.

"Not to worry, sweetheart," he said aloud. "This isn't some kinky game. I'm taping you in so you won't slip out of the sled when I pull it up the stairs."

He tossed the tape roll onto the porch, grabbed the sled line with both hands, and slowly maneuvered the sled up the stairs one step at a time, taking great care not to jar its passenger.

He left the sled next to the wood stove and ran outside for an armload of wood. He soon had the stove refilled and roaring. He made two more trips for firewood before stopping to remove his boots and outerwear.

Wade knelt beside the woman and gently removed the balaclava again. Her face was so white. He could see tiny blue veins under the thin skin of her eyelids and a sprinkle of freckles across her nose. Her lashes were thick and dark against the white of her cheek. He wondered what color her eyes were.

He draped the balaclava neatly over a wooden clothes rack that he kept near the stove for drying.

"Okay, sweetheart. First step is to get the victim out of the wind and cold. You're the vic and you are now out of the wind and cold. So far so good."

He cut the tape off the sled, removed the blanket, and looked down at the unmoving body. "Next step is to remove your clothes without jarring you. That's going to be tougher."

He knelt at her feet and unlaced her boots, taking care to move her legs as little as possible. Lumps of snow fell onto the cabin floor when he pulled off the boots. He peeled off her partially frozen wool socks.

"That must have felt good, all that snow jammed in there. I don't know about you, but I hate cold feet."

When had he become such a chatterbox? He had spoken so little over the last two years that his voice felt rusty from disuse. Somehow he sensed that the woman could hear him, that it was important for her to know she wasn't alone anymore.

Wade placed the felt liners and boots to the side of the stove to dry, hung the socks over the clothes rack, then looked down at the woman again.

"How the hell am I supposed to get those wet clothes off you without moving you, hmmm?" He straddled the sled, placed his fingers inside the waistband of the woman's thin wind pants, and carefully slid them down over slim hips and legs.

"That wasn't too bad. Now you just yell if I'm moving you too much, okay?" He repeated the process with the heavy wool pants and silk long johns, peeling the wet long johns slowly down the woman's long legs and carefully hanging each wet piece of clothing on the clothes rack as he removed it.

"All right. I'm sorry to tell you this but I'm going to have to cut off your sweater and shirt. There's no way I can remove them without jostling you. I can see that they are good quality, and I hate to waste them, but there you have it. Sometimes a man's gotta do what a man's gotta do."

Wade pulled his knife from the sheath he wore on his belt and carefully slit up the center front of the ribbed sweater. He did hate to ruin it, he thought. He appreciated well-made items, no matter what they were.

He sawed through the sweater's thick neck, taking care not to nick the woman. It wasn't going to be enough, he realized, after he'd finished. He needed to slice up each arm as well.

Finally he had shred through the woman's sweater, shirt, and silk underwear top and gently spread them away from her torso. They still lay underneath her body but he didn't see how he could pull them out without moving her too much.

Wade looked down at the nearly naked woman and hesitated. Maybe he could preserve her modesty and leave on her bra and panties. He fingered the silky fabric of her underwear and realized that it was cold and wet. Nope. Everything had to come off.

"Sorry, sweetheart. I'll try not to look."

It had been a long time since he had gazed upon a woman's naked body. He swallowed and cursed at the slight trembling in his hands.

He looked away from the woman. He couldn't do this. He was the last man who should be trying to care for another person. Especially a woman.

He reached deep inside himself to the cold, safe, block of ice that encased what had once been his heart. Wade poked at the ice block and felt relieved that it stood firm; still cold and hard.

But as Wade continued to stare down at the naked woman something stirred in that block of ice. He felt a mix of pity and curiosity. And he couldn't help but notice that the woman possessed a lean, athletic body.

Disgusted with himself, he shook off his thoughts. He needed to get his mind back on treating her hypothermia.

In from the cold—check.

Remove clothes—check.

What's next? Cover with blankets. Got it. But first he needed to get her off the hard sled and onto a softer surface.

He pulled the sled away from the stove and laid out his camping pad and sleeping bag. Although he now spent most of his nights at the cabin in a real bed, when he'd first arrived he used to take frequent overnight hikes into the mountains and still kept his camping gear handy.

Wade slid the sled alongside the makeshift bed and gently lifted the woman onto it. He picked up the soft quilt and held it in front of the stove to warm both sides, then laid it over her and added three wool blankets.

"You should start warming up soon, sweetheart. If I tried to lie next to the wood stove with all those blankets I'd feel as if I was burning up."

He went into the bathroom and returned with his shaving mirror, held it under her nose and waited. "Time to see if you're still alive. Come on honey, breathe for me."

A very faint cloud of moisture appeared on the mirror, so small he would have missed it if he hadn't been waiting for it.

Wade felt a glimmer of hope. Maybe this time, unlike with Susan, he had arrived in time to save a life.

He returned the mirror to his kit and stripped off his clothes. Hesitating for only a few moments, he slid under the blankets next to the woman. He worked his right arm under her neck and gently pulled her into his chest.

He couldn't believe a human body could feel so cold and still be alive.

"Excuse me, sweetheart, but the manual says cuddling up to my bare skin is the best way to get your own heater going," he whispered into her ear. "Please ignore my body part stabbing into your hip.

It's a natural reaction. It's been a long time since I held a naked woman in my arms. I promise I won't make a nuisance of myself. You can trust me."

As Wade held the woman he tried to guess at her story. He judged her age to be somewhere in the late twenties. With those incredible long legs she had to stand nearly six feet tall.

Her fingernails were trimmed square and short and devoid of polish, and her clothing had all been good quality, natural fibers, practical rather than stylish, so she wasn't overly vain or concerned with fashion.

She was lean, but not too, with a pleasantly rounded derriere and round but not over-large breasts.

He was glad that she wasn't model-thin. A thin person would not have survived the exposure to the cold the way she had. He ran his free hand gently up and down her back. She had good muscle tone so she must keep herself in shape he mused.

He pulled his head back and inspected her face. Her broad forehead and narrow chin gave her heart-shaped face intelligence. Her full lips were chapped and still held a bluish tinge. Her strong nose had a small bump that gave her face character, kept her from being cookie-cutter pretty. And the small spattering of freckles across the bridge of her nose and repeated on her left shoulder, made him think of cute little pig-tailed girls.

"You have to pull through, sweetheart," he whispered, "so's I can see what color your eyes are. Don't let me down. I've gone to a lot of trouble for you. Wade Elliot doesn't get naked with many women, you know."

Time passed. Wade fed the fire several times and each time slipped back under the blankets with the woman. If he hadn't been holding a block of ice shaped like a female human he would have been overheated from the blankets and proximity to the stove.

Sometime in the wee morning hours, shivers began to wrack the woman's body. Wade heaved a sigh of relief. The shivers meant her body was beginning to come back to life.

He turned onto his back and rolled her on top of him, stomach to stomach, and wrapped his arms around her. He could relax now. Whoever she was, the woman would survive. Wade tucked her head under his chin and fell asleep.

When he awoke he could tell from the tension in the woman's body that she was awake as well. Wade smiled.

"Welcome back to the land of the living, sweetheart."

4

———————

FAITH DREAMT of down comforters and featherbeds, warm nests that protected her from the relentless wind and cold. She stretched her body and luxuriated in the warmth, glad that her nightmare was over.

She was home again, safe in her small but cheerful, two-bedroom house.

She began to drift back to sleep, then stiffened. How had she gotten home? The last thing she remembered was digging in the snow. Her breath caught. She wasn't home lying in her featherbed.

She shifted a leg experimentally and froze when her thigh rubbed against a strong, hairy thigh.

Where was she? She considered the contours underneath her body.

She was lying naked on top of a naked man!

Faith's pulse began to race. Her naked breasts were pressed against the man's solid chest. She felt stiff, curly hair brush against her nipples and they stiffened in response.

The man's body felt good underneath her, strong and lean and comfortable. Safe.

A deep voice rumbled in her ear.

"Welcome back to the land of the living, sweetheart."

Sweetheart?

"I'm not your sweetheart," Faith rasped. Her throat felt dry and scratchy. She coughed and rolled off the man, taking the blankets with her to cover her nakedness.

"True." He didn't sound too upset by her denial. "But I don't know your name and I had to call you something. I'm Wade Elliot, by the way."

The man lay unmoving. In the faint glow of the wood fire she could see that he watched her through half-lowered eyelids. He seemed unperturbed by his own nudity while he waited for Faith to introduce herself.

She scooted farther away from the disturbingly male naked body until her bare bottom hit the cold floorboards, then busied herself with rearranging the blankets to protect her naked body from the man's gaze and to buy herself time to gather her thoughts.

The silence stretched on. Faith had the sense

that the man before her would wait for as long as it took for her to answer.

"My name is Faith Donahue," she said finally. "How did I get here, and just where *is* here?" Talking scratched her throat and triggered a cough again.

Wade sprang to his feet in a smooth, fluid motion. The firelight from the glass-fronted wood stove silhouetted his body.

Faith couldn't help but notice that he was broad-shouldered and narrow-waisted. And semi-aroused. At least she thought he was semi-aroused. She had so little experience she really couldn't say. She'd never actually seen a naked man before.

She realized she was staring and ducked her head.

Wade heard a low, raspy sound. It surprised him to realize that the sound came from his own throat. When was the last time he had found something amusing enough to laugh aloud?

For some reason it pleased him that the woman, this Faith Donahue, was somewhat shy.

"You need fluids," he said. "I've been keeping water hot on the stove for whenever you woke up. I'll make you some herbal tea and then I have some questions. Mint or chamomile?"

"Mint, please."

A few minutes later Faith sat in a deep and comfortable chair that Wade had pulled next to the stove for her, and sipped her hot tea. The mug warmed her hands and the tea soothed her dry throat.

She still felt cold inside. She felt the warm liquid hit her empty stomach and winced.

The chair was large enough for her to pull her long legs up underneath her. She had dropped the wool blankets and wrapped the pretty quilt around her, leaving only her lower arm holding the mug exposed.

Wade lit a lantern and turned it low before donning a pair of low-slung faded jeans. He sat in a matching chair set a little further from the stove, his long legs stretched out in front of him, crossed at the ankles. He looked relaxed, as if he found half-frozen women every day and brought them home.

Faith studied him as she drank her tea. His ink black hair and bare chest gleamed in the golden firelight. His was not a face one would call handsome, but nonetheless she found it compelling. His intelligent eyes were a deep blue, with tiny wrinkles at the outer corners. She guessed his age to be in the late thirties.

There was a fascinating hardness to Wade's face, as if he had seen and experienced a side of life that most people never knew. His cheekbones were sculpted, not quite gaunt, with a strong, square jaw and a full mouth. She found herself staring at his mouth, wondering how his lips felt. Would they be soft or firm?

One corner of his mouth lifted in a half-smile as if he could read her thoughts. A dimple in his right cheek caught her by surprise. It made him look almost boyish.

Embarrassed, Faith hastily lowered her gaze. Her eyes landed on the curly black hair that covered his chest. She blinked, and followed the dark line of hair down to where it narrowed over his flat belly before disappearing into his jeans.

Faith felt her cheeks flame. Wade Elliot was the sexiest man she had ever seen. She hadn't known that a pair of faded, low-slung jeans could be so alluring. She made a mental note to include a scene like this in her next book.

Wade had more masculinity in one muscled arm than her fiancé Richard possessed in his whole body. Faith recalled how that crisp hair had felt beneath her breasts. Her nipples tightened in response.

Richard. She was getting married on Saturday. The thought brought her back to the present. Guilt washed through her. Wade and Richard were two very different men. She had no business comparing them. Richard had a fine mind, he was a scholar, not an outdoorsman like the man sitting before her.

She swallowed more tea as she considered the

gravity of her situation. Here she sat, naked but for the quilt, in a strange man's cabin in the backwoods of northern Maine. What if Wade was a criminal of some sort, hiding out from the law in this remote cabin?

She shook her head slightly and discarded that notion immediately. If Wade was a fugitive he wouldn't have gone to the trouble of saving her life.

Wade sat quietly and watched and waited. Dealing with Faith was a bit like dealing with a wild animal—be quiet and make no sudden moves to startle it.

He allowed the woman the time to inspect him. She wasn't going anywhere. He had plenty of time to learn her story. The fact that he was interested in learning about her didn't escape his attention. It had been several years since he had felt curiosity about another person.

It pleased and impressed him that she had not displayed fear at waking up naked in a strange place with a naked stranger. The hand that held the tea mug had stopped shaking once her body warmed. Her eyes were curious but not frightened.

He knew she was at a severe disadvantage without her clothing. He had not offered her anything to wear, intending to exploit that, to keep her slightly off balance until she answered his questions.

Once a cop, always a cop, he thought ruefully.

It didn't seem to matter how long he was away from the job.

He set his own empty mug down on the floor beside his chair and pulled in his legs, then leaned forward, resting his elbows on his thighs and loosely clasping his hands.

"Okay, Mrs. Donahue, why don't you tell me how I came to find you nearly dead from hypothermia, and start from the beginning. We have plenty of time."

"Miss. I'm not married. Not yet, anyway."

Faith sipped at her tea and wondered how much she needed to tell Wade Elliot to satisfy his curiosity. The beginning of her ugly story started way back in her childhood, but she honestly didn't want to get into all of that old history.

"My sister and I decided to do some winter camping."

Wade's eyes narrowed but he said nothing.

He had the most beautiful blue eyes and thick, black lashes, Faith thought, momentarily distracted. She wished he would leave her alone so she could simply stare at him and drink in his male perfection.

Wade made a rolling motion with one hand. "Go on."

"We made camp late. When I woke up my sister was gone." Faith shrugged. "That's pretty much it."

Wade's eyebrows rose in disbelief. "That's it? I know you came in on a snow machine, I heard it pass by twice two night's ago and saw the track the next morning. How did your sister manage to take off without you knowing?"

He'd save the question of *why* a sister would even do such a thing. There was obviously a story there.

Faith wrinkled her nose. "I'm not sure. It does sound a little weird, doesn't it? I was feeling pretty tired. I had driven from Falmouth—that's just north of Portland—to Greenville, and then we took my snowmobile from there to wherever here is. We set up the tent and drank a bottle of champagne. At least I think we did. I know I had a glass."

She shrugged one quilt-covered shoulder. "It hit me pretty hard, I guess. That's all I remember. Like I told you—I went to sleep and when I woke up Hope was gone. She drove my snow machine from Greenville so she already had the keys."

Wade looked at Faith for a long moment. Turquoise, he realized. Her eyes were an unusual shade of bright green-blue and slightly tilted up at the outer corners, giving her face an exotic, feline look.

He leaned back into the chair and steepled his fingers, tapping the index fingers together, a habit he had developed while on the force that helped him think.

"Why would your sister leave you to die?"

Faith's hand jerked, sending tea spilling over the lip of the mug and onto her wrist. She licked the liquid off her arm.

Wade watched the delicate pink tongue and tried not to think of how it would taste in his mouth. He really had gone too long without a woman, he thought with disgust. What the hell was he supposed to do with her? He was here for peace and solitude and she was definitely disturbing them.

"Kill me? Why-why do you say that Hope was trying to kill me?" The same conclusion had occurred to Faith, but somehow hearing the words spoken aloud by Wade Elliot made them more real. More terrible.

Wade's eyes bore into her own. "Why else would your sister have abandoned you to the elements forty miles from the nearest town? Is this some sick game you two play?"

"What? Game? No! No." Faith shook her head. "Unfortunately it's no game," she mumbled.

Of course it wasn't a game. Hope had set out to kill her. Finally, after a lifetime of torment, her sister had gone for it all.

Seeing the misery in the woman's face, Wade

decided to back off. He'd get the story eventually. There was definitely something there.

He stood and reached for the tea mug. "Let me get you another. The manual says that hypothermia victims need lots of warm fluids to warm their internal organs."

"Do you have any soup instead? I'm famished. I haven't eaten since the burger I picked up in Greenville two and a half days ago."

"Yeah, I have soup. It'll take a few minutes to warm it. Drink another cup of tea while it heats. You want chamomile this time?"

Faith thanked him when he placed another blessedly hot mug in her hands. She could feel her body beginning to thaw out.

She ignored the sharp bursts of pain as her nerve endings came alive again and resisted the urge to check her toes for frostbite. She could wiggle them so they weren't dead. She felt reluctant to bare any part of her body in front of Wade again.

The fact that she wanted to do just that frightened her. That she wanted to feel his naked body pressed against hers again terrified her.

"I need to get home," she said. "I'm going to be married on Saturday. Can you take me back to Greenville today?"

Wade turned from stirring a pot of soup on the wood stove.

"No, Miss Donahue, I can't take you to Greenville today. I have only one pair of snowshoes. No snowmobile, I'm afraid. You're stuck here for the remainder of the winter."

Faith frowned over her mug of tea. "All right. I'll just use your phone to call my fiancé to come get me. Do you have GPS coordinates for this place?"

Wade said nothing as he filled a new mug with chicken and wild rice soup and handed it to Faith along with a spoon. He took the tea mug from her and stood looking down at his unexpected and unwanted houseguest.

"Where do you think we are, Miss Donahue?" he asked. "There are no phone lines, and no cell towers nearby. No, when I said we're stuck here for the duration of the winter, I meant just that. I'm afraid you'll have to reschedule your wedding for next spring, when we can walk and canoe out of here."

Faith's mouth dropped open. She almost dropped the mug of soup. She hurriedly set it down on the floor and then stood. She wrapped the quilt tightly around her body and stepped closer to Wade, until they were standing mere inches apart. She didn't have to bend her head back very far to look him in the eye.

"That's unacceptable, Mr. Elliot. I *have* to be in Falmouth by ten in the morning on Saturday.

I'm getting married. Do you really expect me to believe that you have no way to contact the outside world? What if you become ill or have an accident?"

Wade looked into Faith Donahue's eyes. Green, he thought. They turn green when she's angry.

"I heard you, Miss Donahue, but there's nothing I can do. I don't have contact with the outside world and that's the way I like it. I'm not happy about having a houseguest, not to mention the strain an extra mouth will put on my supplies, but it seems I have no choice.

"I suggest you make the best of it. If your fiancé loves you he'll be happy to wait for you and marry you after the ice goes out. Or else he'll come looking for you. I certainly would."

Now why had he said that? Wade wondered, disgusted with himself.

Fear flashed briefly in Faith's eyes.

That's interesting, mused Wade. I wonder what this woman is afraid of? Perhaps she isn't as sure of her future husband's love as she'd like to believe.

"I see," Faith said stiffly. "And just when does the ice go out, may I ask?"

Wade shrugged one shoulder. "Who knows? I don't keep a calendar. Spring will arrive when it arrives, as it always does."

Faith's lips made a moue of annoyance. Her eyes narrowed. "I don't accept that. Let me borrow your snowshoes. I'll hike out of here and return them when I retrieve my snowmobile."

"Huh. Not a chance. How am I supposed to get around while you're gone? And why should I trust you? You could take off with my shoes and I'll never see you again."

Faith drew herself up and raised her chin. Indignation and annoyance showed clearly in her eyes. "I assure you Mr. Elliot, I am a very honest person. If I say that I will return your snowshoes, then I will return your snowshoes."

Wade gave the woman standing before him a considering look. "And who's to say that you can find your way out of here, Miss Donahue?" he asked softly. "What happens if you get lost in the woods again? Then you'll die and I'll never get my snowshoes back."

Faith stepped closer to him. He was uncomfortably aware of her nakedness under his quilt.

"I'm sorry, but you'll have to resign yourself to staying here with me until we can both hike out of here. I promise to return you to the loving bosom of your family as soon as possible."

Faith realized that in her anger she had moved even closer to Wade, until her bare toes were touching Wade's bare toes. That brought back the memory of waking up naked on top of his warm, firm body. Scowling, she took a step back.

"I need some clothes."

"Certainly." Wade grabbed Faith's silk underwear off the clothes drying rack. The fabric felt cool and smooth in his rough hands. He held them out.

"I had to destroy your tops to get them off your body. Sorry. I'll get you one of my shirts to wear. After you finish your soup you may take the bed. Your body needs rest to finish recovering from your ordeal. We'll talk more when you wake."

"What more is there to discuss?" Faith snapped, snatching the silk long johns from Wade's hand. "You won't let me leave and that's all I want to talk about."

Wade's eyes hardened to the deep blue of a cold northern lake.

"You still haven't told me why your sister tried to murder you, Miss Donahue."

5

FAITH DRESSED in her long underwear, thick warm socks and a borrowed shirt, finished off the soup, and crawled gratefully into Wade's bed. Despite her tumultuous thoughts, she fell asleep in only a few minutes.

She woke, hungry again, but warm and very comfortable. She stretched and looked around the tidy cabin. Wade Elliot was a neat man, she decided. There were no articles of clothing, dirty dishes, or papers laying about. The mugs she had used earlier were washed and drying upside down in a dish rack by the sink.

She saw no sign of Wade.

Sunlight streamed through the window by the bed. Faith propped herself up on the pillows and took advantage of his absence to inspect the large, one-room cabin.

She liked it, she thought with approval. The bed sat between two windows. A thick, braided rug in shades of blue and brown and red covered the center of the cabin floor. Matching deep blue leather reading chairs sat facing the wood stove. The chairs were well-worn, showing years of use that only leather can hold up to.

The glass-fronted wood stove sat on a stone hearth. More rounded, gray stone covered a large portion of the cabin's back wall before narrowing down to a chimney that disappeared into the pine-paneled ceiling.

Every inch of solid wall space held floor-to-ceiling bookshelves. They were filled with neat stacks of books, magazines, and carvings of animals. There were no photos of people. Faith wondered why that was.

The opposite back corner of the room had been walled off into what she hoped was a bathroom. The thought of having to use an outhouse—baring her bottom outside in the bitter cold again—made her shiver.

Now that she had thought of the bathroom she couldn't ignore the pressure on her bladder. She threw aside the blankets, noting that Wade had covered her with two of the wool blankets in addition to the quilt. He may be large and tough, but somewhere inside that amazing body was a person with a heart.

To Faith's relief, the small corner room was indeed a bathroom, complete with a glass shower stall, a pedestal sink, and a washer-dryer combo stacked in one corner.

Faith gasped with horror when she caught a glimpse of herself in the small mirror over the sink.

Her thick curly hair hung in greasy clumps about her shoulders and her eyes were shadowed and bruised-looking. Her freckles stood out in stark relief from her pale skin. She rubbed the bump on her nose absently.

She looked over her shoulder at the shower stall. A pile of neatly folded towels filled a shelf over the toilet. Faith turned on the shower and flipped the latch on the bathroom door. She emerged fifteen minutes later, clean and fresh, and feeling far more able to apply her mind to the problem of how to get home in time for her wedding.

When Wade returned he found her sitting next to the wood stove sipping tea. He dropped an armload of wood into the woodbox and removed his outerwear, hanging everything on a row of hooks by the door.

"Hungry?" he asked as he moved into the kitchen area.

"Famished! Do you cook?" Faith got up from

the chair and moved to the square oak dining table.

"Yeah. I'd starve to death otherwise. The nearest take-out is forty miles away and they don't deliver by snowmobile."

Faith watched him carefully peel several strips of bacon from a large slab and lay them side by side in a cast iron fry pan.

The wood stove fire popped. The bacon sizzled and filled the cabin with the mouth-watering smell of frying pig. She heard a crow call outside the cabin. Another answered. Sunlight streamed through the windows.

A sense of peace came over Faith, taking her by surprise. When was the last time she had felt truly relaxed?

Never, she thought with a wry grin. She had never been able to let down her guard with Hope around. Even in her little house she never knew when Hope would simply show up or call. It didn't matter what hour of the day or night— Hope had never recognized Faith's personal boundaries.

No, that wasn't entirely fair, she amended. The fact was that she had never stood up to her sister. She didn't have to answer her phone, or allow Hope into her house, but she did. They were sisters after all. No matter what Hope did, Faith always gave her another chance to be a real sister, another chance to show Faith that Hope cared about her.

Faith took a deep breath and let it out in an audible sigh.

Wade set a wide shallow pot of water to simmer and sliced bread for toast. "So," he said, watching her from the corner of his eye. "Why would your sister—what's her name?—want you dead?"

He kept his tone as neutral as possible and resisted looking directly at the woman sitting at his table. He wanted answers but he wasn't ready to put hard pressure on her—not yet anyway.

"Hope. My sister's name is Hope. She's my older sister by thirteen months. Hope is . . . Hope is just Hope." Faith shrugged one shoulder and ran a finger around the rim of her mug.

She found it difficult to describe her sister. Nobody who met Hope had ever believed her version of the sister from hell. They took one look at her beautiful sister and concluded that Faith was the one who was messed in the head.

"She competes with me for everything," Faith finally said. "It doesn't matter what it is—my favorite doll, our mother's love, the cat's attention, grades in school. She has to be smarter and prettier —which she is. Hope is both scary intelligent and beautiful."

Faith struggled to find the words to explain something she didn't really understand herself.

"She's been like that as far back as I can remember, but after our father divorced Mom and moved to California to marry another woman, Hope got worse. Before Dad left she didn't seem as needy. Afterwards, she demanded all the attention. It didn't matter who it was from. Mom. My friends. Teachers.

"She used to tell outrageous stories, stories that made me look bad. She'd blame me for the things that she did and loved it when I was punished for them."

"Your mother couldn't see what she was doing?"

Faith shook her head. "In a nutshell—no. You'd have to meet Hope to understand. She looks and acts like an angel, except with me. So everyone assumes that she is one."

She pushed the tea mug away. "I can't answer your question because I don't know why my sister hates me. Can we talk about something else?"

Wade cracked three eggs into the simmering water. Before long he set a plate with a bacon and poached egg sandwich in front of Faith and two for himself. He poured them both fresh mugs of tea and sat down to eat.

Faith took a bite of the sandwich. The bread and bacon were crispy and the egg yolk soft and runny. The combination felt like heaven in her mouth.

"Oh my god, this is so good. Better than any breakfast sandwich from Mickey Dee's. Where'd you learn to cook?"

"My mother feels that everyone should be able to whip up a few good meals so they won't starve if left on their own. She doesn't believe in fast food joints. Swears they're one of the reasons there are so many criminals and drug addicts in the country."

Faith stopped with the sandwich halfway to her mouth. "What does fast food have to do with criminal behavior?"

"Something to do with the way bad cholesterol acts on the brain and too much meat makes men aggressive. You'd have to ask her if you want to understand it. Back to your sister. Did she drink any of the champagne?"

"Sure. She opened the bottle outside the tent while I set up our sleeping gear, then came in with two glasses and we sat and drank them together. Why?"

Instead of answering, Wade looked out the front windows, off into the distance. He waited for Faith to finish her breakfast. "And you only drank the one glass and then fell asleep?"

"I think so. I honestly don't remember. Again, why?"

"I suspect that your sister drugged you, Miss Donahue. It sounds as if she slipped a roofie into your drink."

Faith's mouth fell open. She couldn't believe that Hope would give her the date rape drug. Hope could be an unreasonable bitch, but to drug her own sister? Faith didn't want to believe it.

"Why would she do that? Why would she drug me?"

Wade gave her a hard look and waited. Let her figure it out for herself, he thought. She wouldn't believe him if he just told her.

Faith stood and began to pace the room. "Why?" she repeated. "I mean, if she wanted to kill me, why try to kill me that way? And why now?"

She stopped and jammed her fists on her hips. Tapped a toe. Frowned at Wade who sat placidly eating his breakfast.

Faith pointed a finger at him. "All she has to do is ignore me and I'd be out of her life. No, you're wrong, Mr. Elliot. I don't know why she abandoned me here, but I can't believe she'd drug me in order to leave me here to die. Something happened so that she had to leave and she couldn't wake me. That has to be it."

Faith resumed her pacing. She stopped by the windows that looked onto a front porch and a frozen lake below. Was it a lake? Maybe it was the bog she had stumbled upon.

She knew her denial sounded weak. It sounded weak to her own ears. Her stomach clenched. Deep inside she knew the truth. Wade's theory was plausible. It was even the most likely explanation, but she didn't want to believe that her only sibling could be that cold-blooded.

She shuddered as it hit home how lucky she had been. If Wade hadn't seen her she would be nothing more than a frozen lump in the snow. She turned and looked at her savior. His blue eyes watched her steadily.

"Okay," she said reluctantly, "maybe I can buy the roofie theory. One glass of champagne shouldn't have put me under the way it did, no matter how tired I was. But why? Why would Hope try to kill me?"

"What do you have that Hope wants?" Wade asked softly.

"Nothing! I-oh. No." She shook her head. "No. I won't believe that she wants Richard. She *likes* Richard. He's the only person she hasn't tried to chase out of my life."

"That right there should send up warning flags."

Faith walked over to one of the leather chairs and plopped down. "It's the only explanation that makes sense, isn't it?"

She dropped her head into her hands. "I should have known things were going too smoothly. I was so happy when she started to behave like a normal sister. It never occurred to me that it was an act."

Faith picked up her head and glared at Wade. "All right, I admit it, I was stupid."

Wade held out his palms. "I never said you were stupid. You wanted to believe your sister had changed. I can understand that. It speaks well of you that you continued to look for the good in her." Even though Hope sounded like a true bitch, he added silently.

"You don't have to say it. I know you're thinking it."

"Most people don't change after behaving one way their entire lives, Miss Donahue."

Faith slumped back in the chair and stuck her legs out in front of her. She knew that Wade had a point, but she hated to admit that Hope had sucked her in with her nice sister act. God, but she was pathetic—to still want Hope's love after all the things that her sister had done to her.

Faith jumped up from the chair and stalked over to the table. She placed her palms flat on its surface and leaned into Wade.

"You're right. All the more reason for me to get out of here. Hope is up to something. You *have* to lend me your snowshoes. *Please.* I'll hike to Greenville and call Richard to come get me. I promise to return them before he takes me back to Falmouth."

"I can't do that, Miss Donahue. Do you even know which direction to go in? You'll be lost in no time. I'd be sending you out to your death. I'm sorry, I truly am, but if Richard loves you he'll get the truth from Hope and come looking for you. It would be best if you waited for him here."

Faith's spirits rose. "You really think he'll come for me?"

"It's what I'd do," Wade replied. He looked up at the large turquoise eyes staring down at him and the mass of mahogany curls dancing around her shoulders. Her hair gleamed with red and gold highlights that blended in with the deeper reddish-brown.

He wondered if his hands would feel the heat from those highlights. The desire to bury his hands and face in Faith's hair swept over him.

Pretty hair. Beautiful expressive eyes. He re-called the way her athletic, naked body had felt stretched out on top of him.

Wade cleared his throat and pushed his chair back from the table. He gathered the breakfast dishes and set them in the sink. Miss Donahue was spoken for, he reminded himself, and obviously anxious to marry her Richard. He had strict rules about poaching on another man's territory.

Faith washed the dishes while Wade carried in armloads of wood until the wood box towered with neatly split lengths of firewood.

"Why so much wood?" she asked.

"There's a storm coming."

Faith walked to a front window and looked out at the clear blue sky and the sun reflecting off the wide expanse of snow below. She turned back to Wade with a puzzled expression.

"It's a beautiful day. What makes you think we're going to get a storm?" She looked at him suspiciously. "You have a way to connect with the outside world, don't you? You heard a weather report."

Wade walked over to an instrument hanging on the wall near the stove and tapped it.

"See for yourself. The barometer's falling. My grandfather called days like this weather breeders. No wind, high pressure. Clear skies. Weather breeders suck in low pressure. The wind will pick up tonight. I saw the clouds on the horizon when I took my morning hike. That means there's moisture in the atmosphere. We'll get snow, I promise you."

Wade pulled on his outer wear and turned to Faith. "I'm going after the log I left behind yesterday. I'll bring back your tent. I should be back before nightfall. Help yourself to anything you'd like to read or eat and try to get more rest. Your body needs it."

Faith watched Wade shoe down the slope in front of the cabin, pulling the empty sled behind him. She turned and looked around the cabin. Did

she really believe that Wade had no means of contacting the outside world? What if he was hurt? He
had to have a way to call for help.

She didn't know why he would lie to her, but
she couldn't believe that he lived here in complete
isolation. She began to search the cabin for Wade's
cell phone.

6

WADE BREATHED IN THE CRISP, cold air as he trudged steadily down the bog. He took off his hat and stuffed it into his pack. He loved days like this. He almost felt at peace in them.

He thought about the woman back in the cabin and the story she had told him. His instincts told him that she was telling the truth. The problem was that he wasn't sure he trusted his instincts anymore. He hadn't trusted them since he had been forced to retire.

Did she really have an evil sister, he wondered? Faith's story sounded plausible on the surface. Lord knows there were plenty of dysfunctional families out there. He had seen them every day working homicide. Too often, the victim and killer were members of the same family.

A beautiful or handsome face was no guarantee that the person behind it possessed an honest, good soul.

Faith came across as honest and a little naive. Wade found that he wanted to believe her.

He would keep chipping away at her story until he felt sure he knew the truth. He had time. Faith Donahue wasn't going anywhere until spring.

Wade made good time getting back to where he'd left the log. He rolled it onto the sled and secured it, then headed across the bog for Faith's tent. He hadn't wanted to come out here today but the pending snowstorm had forced him to retrieve the items before they were buried in the blizzard.

He broke down the tent poles and rolled them inside the tent and stuffed the whole package under the log to keep it from blowing away.

The sun dipped low over the mountains to the west. It would be dark soon. Knowing that a woman waited for his return made him feel strange. Good, but strange.

He looked forward to seeing her again, he realized. It was more than the puzzle she represented; he found her intelligent and attractive. He smiled to himself and shook his head. Life was full of surprises.

Wade trudged close to the west side of the bog, watching for fresh tracks in the snow. He'd love to see the secretive lynx again. It was such a beautiful animal.

The ice cracked beneath him. Too late, he knew that he had crossed a thin patch in the ice, probably formed over one of the many springs that fed the bog. He tried to move faster across the thin ice but it gave way beneath him. Wade fell into the frigid water up to his shoulders.

He gasped as the frigid water soaked through his clothing. The heavy sled slid in behind him, trapping the back edges of his snowshoes.

His first thought was to release his boots from the shoes and leave them, but he quickly dismissed that idea. Without the snowshoes he'd never make it back to the cabin before freezing to death.

He pushed his right leg forward experimentally, hoping the shoe would slide out from beneath the sled. It didn't move. He twisted his torso and tried to pull the sled up by the harness line but couldn't get a decent grip on it.

He had no choice. He had to remove the snowshoes and then work them free.

Wade removed his gloves and tossed them onto the ice shelf, took a deep breath and plunged down into the murky water. He fumbled with the snowshoe fittings, thankful that he had retired his old-fashioned set of shoes and invested in a new, lightweight pair with quick-release fittings.

His fingers quickly grew numb and began to

ache. He got one boot free and had to come up for air. The shock of the cold air on his wet head brought home the seriousness of his situation. He drew a deep breath and bent back down into the water. This time it felt almost balmy compared to the air above the surface.

Wade freed his second boot and turned around so he faced the sled. He reached down and grasped the front edge with one hand while he tugged on a snowshoe with the other. The shoe came free. He stood and shouted in triumph.

He pulled the second shoe free and climbed onto the log. The extra height gave him what he needed to fling his body onto the thicker ice. He laid in the snow for a brief moment and pushed to his knees. His wet clothes stiffened as they began to freeze.

Time was of the essence. Wearing wet clothing in single-digit temperatures would rob his body of heat fast. His fingers already refused to work. He put them in his mouth to warm them, got the right snowshoe on and repeated the process for the left.

"Go Wade, go as fast as you can," he muttered to himself. His clothes were already solidifying. He broke into an awkward shuffle and concentrated on putting one foot in front of the other.

"What a fool, Wade old boy. You weren't paying attention." He blamed the distraction of his pretty houseguest for the lapse. He knew that the bog had springs and dangerous patches of ice. He knew better than to hike so close to the edge where the ice tended to be thinner.

"Move, Wade, move. Don't stop moving. If you want to live you have to keep moving."

~

Faith searched every nook and cranny inside the cabin. She pulled out every book and looked behind it, opened every drawer and removed its contents, searched the kitchen cabinets and underneath the mattress and chair cushions. She even checked the chimney rocks for hidden hidey-holes.

She found two sets of carving chisels in the set of drawers under one bookcase. One set was small, the type a carver would use for fine work. The other, much larger, was still in its original packaging.

So, Wade had carved the animals that decorated the shelves. Faith picked up a carving of a bear and inspected it. The detail was exquisite, she thought. Wade could easily sell them in a gallery. She set the bear back in its spot and looked around the cabin with a sense of defeat.

She had searched everywhere. Wade had been telling her the truth. There was no phone, and therefore no way to call Richard. Her only option was to steal Wade's snowshoes and hike out of here.

She could do it. She had found a photo album filled with old pictures of the original cabin. In one photo a car sat next to the cabin. Cars needed roads. Granted, the road to the cabin was most likely a minimum maintenance road, which meant it was not plowed and rarely graded, but it would eventually lead her to a main road.

The forest could also have taken it over completely since the photo was taken.

She pulled on her boots and walked out onto the front porch. The right porch edge looked out onto a small clearing surrounded by thick-set spruce trees. A wire fence surrounded the clearing. A vegetable garden perhaps, she wondered?

She could picture Wade gardening, his vegetables growing in precise, neat rows. He would garden the same way he did everything else, she decided: with single-minded focus and thoroughness.

She wondered if he made love the same way.

The thought came out of the blue and surprised her. She had no business wondering how Wade Elliot made love. She was engaged to be married in only a couple days.

Still, the thought of making love with Wade gave her a warm thrill unlike anything she had ever experienced before.

Richard never inspired those feelings. She shied

away from the thought and the instant guilt that filled her. Wade and Richard were two very different men. It was unfair to compare them to one another.

She turned away from the garden and walked to the opposite edge of the porch and leaned out over the railing. There was a small cleared area on this side of the cabin as well, but what excited her was a narrow, snow-covered break in the trees. Elation coursed through her, quickly followed by guilt at what she planned to do.

Leaving Wade stranded without snowshoes to get around made her feel bad, but missing her own wedding made her feel worse. She straightened her back and clumped back inside the cabin.

She didn't want to examine why she held doubts that Richard would come looking for her. He must love her—after all, he had asked her to marry him, hadn't he? Wasn't that proof of his love? She didn't need Richard to traipse all over the Maine woods looking for her to prove anything.

She pushed aside the niggling little thought that Wade would do whatever it took to retrieve the woman he loved.

Wade and Richard were very different men, she reminded herself again firmly. Wade was big and strong and capable. He was the type of man who ran into burning buildings to save someone who was trapped.

Richard on the other hand was an intellectual. A gentle man. He would call for help if he saw a building on fire.

Two very different men.

A girl has to do what a girl has to do, Faith told herself. She would return the snowshoes as soon as Richard met her in Greenville with her snow machine. And she'd bring Wade a gift as well, to show her appreciation for his saving her life.

Faith fed the fire and set the soup pot on to reheat. She whipped up a batch of cornbread to go with the soup. A small peace offering for the wrong she was about to do.

She couldn't put off leaving even another day. It might take her two, or even three days to hike to Greenville if she couldn't hitch a ride. She had to contact Richard before Saturday.

As soon as Wade headed into the shower she would take his snowshoes and set off.

Somehow she knew that he would shower. Wade was a man who took care of things, including himself. She had noticed how pleasant he smelled —a combination of woodsmoke and pine and fresh air underlaid with a faint muskiness that she suspected was his male scent.

Faith set her boots by the door along with her wool pants and wind pants. She would have to move fast when the time came. She tucked her mittens and goggles into her balaclava and stuffed them into Wade's windbreaker. A down vest hung beneath the windbreaker. She would take that as well, she decided, and return everything to him as soon as possible.

She felt an unexpected reluctance to leave this place. Maybe after she was married she could convince Richard to do some winter camping and they could come back here.

She knew as soon as she had the thought that it would never happen. Richard hated the outdoors. Her fiancé preferred libraries, colleges and universities, historic societies. Museums.

Like her, Richard was a writer, but unlike her, he had yet to sell any of his work. Romantic suspense sold much better than historical biographies.

Faith had gently suggested that perhaps he should turn his attention to characters that a reader might find interesting, but he held firm to the notion that the world needed to be informed about the lives of the dry, obscure subjects that he focused on.

Faith pulled a book off the shelves and sat by the fire to read and wait for Wade's return. Twilight arrived, and then night fell. Still no sign of Wade.

She rose and lit the lantern and began to pace the cabin floor. He'd said he would return before nightfall. She was growing worried. The wind had picked up as Wade had predicted, and thick clouds obscured the moon and stars. She pulled on her boots and Wade's windbreaker and stepped out onto the porch to see if she could spot him coming across the bog.

It took her several minutes to spy his body lying at the bottom of the steps.

7

"WADE? Oh my god, Wade! What happened?"

Faith flew down the steps and knelt beside Wade's shivering body. His clothes were frozen solid.

She fumbled with the icy snowshoe bindings but the ice was too thickly encrusted over the release mechanism. She pounded her fist on the binding but it wouldn't release. Faith unlaced one of Wade's boots and slipped it off his foot with the snowshoe attached.

She tossed them aside. She'd bring them inside later after she took care of Wade. She quickly removed the second boot and shoe, cringing when water slopped out of the boot.

"Wade." Faith shook his shoulder and spoke

into his ear. "Wade! I have to get you inside the cabin. Can you walk?"

"N-n-n-no."

Faith almost swooned with relief when Wade answered. If he could talk then he wasn't dead—yet.

"That answer is unacceptable, Wade Elliot. A big, strong man like you should have no problem climbing up a couple of steps. Don't be a baby. Come on, I'll even help you."

She rolled Wade onto his back, wrapped her arms around his shoulders, and pulled him to a seated position. His icy clothing crackled. The cold wafted off him into her face. His eyebrows and eyelashes were white and stiff with ice.

Faith swallowed her fear. She had to get him inside the warm cabin immediately.

"All right, big guy," she said aloud. "Put your arm over my shoulders. When I say three we're going to stand and go up the steps. Ready? Three!" Faith pulled with all her might.

Wade rolled back onto his side and struggled to get his feet under him. He knew that if he didn't get inside the cabin he would die. He felt so weak, like a newborn animal with no muscles to speak of. If Faith's arm hadn't been supporting him he would've fallen straight down again. He had used up every ounce of strength he possessed getting himself this far.

He leaned on Faith and focused on her encouraging words.

"That's right. I knew any guy who looks like you do couldn't be a wussy kind of guy. One more step and we'll be inside. You can do it. Lift your left leg, Wade. There! Great work."

A blast of warm air hit Wade's face as they entered the cabin. He almost wept with joy.

Faith led him toward the wood stove and leaned him against the back of one chair. She ran back to close the cabin door, then returned and peeled off his stockings. She peeled off his pants and long underwear, gasping when she saw how Wade's thighs were red and abraded from the frozen fabric.

She quickly removed the remainder of Wade's clothing and grabbed a blanket from the bed. She wrapped it around his shivering body.

"What happened? Can you tell me?" she asked as she dumped his clothing into the sink to melt.

"Hit-hit a weak p-p-patch. F-f-fell thr-thr-through. L-l-lucky g-got out."

Faith piled the remainder of the blankets beside the stove to warm, then began undressing. She talked, babbled really, to hide her discomfort at undressing in front of a man she barely knew.

"I may regret this, but I know nothing about hypothermia so I'm going to follow your lead. Surely I can sacrifice my modesty to save the life of someone who saved mine. The important thing is to get you warmed up."

She fed the fire, replaced the warmed blankets on the bed, and led Wade to it. She helped him into the bed and crawled in after him. Faith wrapped her arms around Wade. The coldness of his skin shocked Faith. She drew him tight to her and repressed a shiver.

"No funny business now," she said, trying to make a joke. "I'm an engaged woman, remember."

Bad jokes were her way of hiding her fear. Wade's condition scared her. He had only Faith to help him and she knew less than nothing about how to treat hypothermia.

What an arrogant fool she had been. Who went winter camping without learning the basics about hypothermia? She made a silent vow to learn everything there was to learn about the subject when she got home. Maybe she'd include it in the plot of her next book.

For now, all she remembered about how Wade had treated her own hypothermia was waking up naked on top of Wade's naked body.

"The least I can do is share my body heat with you," she said aloud. "I'll have you know I've never said that to anyone before. You're my first naked man. Sad, but true."

Wade snuggled into her arms. "D-d-died and gg-gone to heaven," he stammered. He pressed into her and promptly fell asleep.

"So much for my big getaway," muttered Faith into his wet hair. She couldn't leave Wade in this condition. Not until she knew he would be all right. She settled against him and soon fell asleep.

Hours later—how many she had no way of knowing—Faith woke. She was burning up. She started to fling the blankets aside, then remembered Wade.

He had pulled away from her and lay on his back, his arms flung outside of the blankets. The heat was coming off him in waves, she realized. She got to her knees and placed her cheek against his forehead.

Wade's body burned with fever. Faith crawled from the bed and put on her long johns and the borrowed shirt. She tended the fire, then filled a bowl with cool water and grabbed a washcloth from the bathroom.

Setting the bowl on the bedside table, she wet and wrung out the cloth and placed it on Wade's forehead. He mumbled something and groaned. From too cold to too hot, she thought. What the hell was she supposed to do?

When the water in the bowl became too warm to do any good she replaced it. While carrying a fresh bowl of cool water back to the bed her eyes lit on one of the bookshelves. It held a variety of reference books. She had noticed them during her search of the cabin, but hadn't paid particular attention to the individual books.

Faith set the bowl of water on the bedside table and returned to the bookshelf. There were books on electrical wiring, plumbing, solar power—was Wade thinking of adding solar power to the cabin? — gardening, small engine repair, carpentry— nothing on medicine.

Okay, don't panic, Faith, she told herself. What do you know about fevers? Think! Faith paced the floor in front of the bookshelves.

Sometimes a fever is the body's way of fighting off infection. Wade had been submersed in the bog. He probably got water up his nose or in his mouth. Water that contains zillions of little microbes. He could be fighting anything.

What did she do when she had a temperature? She took aspirin and slept.

Faith whirled around and raced to the bathroom. She found a bottle of Tylenol in a first aid kit. No thermometer. The Tylenol wasn't aspirin. but it might help ease Wade's aches. She grabbed a mug of water and carried the Tylenol and water to the bedside table so they would be handy when Wade woke up.

Faith tried to sit on the edge of the bed but Wade was thrashing around, so she dragged one of the reading chairs next to the bed and sat in it instead. Whenever he calmed she continued to place the cool wet cloth over his forehead, wiping his cheeks and neck and arms, waiting for him to become lucid enough to take the Tylenol.

"Water."

The raspy croak woke Faith. She had curled up in the reading chair and covered herself with Wade's parka. She jumped up and grabbed the bottle of Tylenol and the mug of water.

"I'm so glad you're awake. I was getting pretty worried about you."

Wade looked at her with feverish eyes. His skin was covered in a clammy sheen of sweat. He tried to lift his head to the mug but couldn't manage it.

"Here, let me help you." Faith scooted onto the bed next to him and gently lifted his head. She held the mug to his cracked lips. Water dribbled out of the side of his mouth and she dabbed at it with the cloth.

"Funny how people revert to acting like infants when they're sick, isn't it?" she said lightly. "Take these pills, they'll help you feel better."

Wade swallowed the pills and weakly pushed her hand away after he'd taken a little more water. He muttered something she couldn't understand and closed his eyes.

"You're welcome. Get some more rest. Hopefully the Tylenol will help your fever."

The next day dawned without the sun. The sky,

a cold, metallic gray, soon began to spit small flakes of snow. As the morning progressed the snowflakes grew larger and thicker until Faith could no longer see down the slope to the bog.

She had been feeding the wood stove from the pile of wood that Wade had carried in the previous day. The woodbox was now almost empty. She knew she couldn't let the fire die. She brought in the snowshoes, still attached to Wade's boots, and set them next to the wood stove to melt off the ice crusting the fittings.

As soon as she was able to free the snowshoes from the boots, Faith pulled on her wool pants and one of Wade's jackets and went looking for the woodpile. She found a small mountain of split wood covered with snow on the edge of the clearing that abutted the lane into the cabin.

Why hadn't Wade made the woodpile closer, easier to reach? Faith looked back at the cabin. She could barely see it through the thickly falling snow.

She sighed. Although the wood wasn't that far away, only forty feet or so, it would take a lot more time and energy to carry armloads of wood to the cabin from there.

She turned to her left and stared at the narrow opening between the thick evergreens—the end of the lane that in to the cabin. Freedom and Richard lay that way.

She looked back toward the cabin again. A man she knew absolutely nothing about lay inside.

She had the snowshoes. And she had Wade's parka. He was in no shape to come after her. She could head for Greenville right now and with luck be there within a day or two. She turned again and stared unseeing at the woodpile, debating what to do.

This was her chance to make her escape.

Faith took several steps toward the opening and stopped.

It didn't feel like an escape; it felt as if she was running away from someone who desperately needed her help.

She made a frustrated sound in her throat and turned back, loaded her arms with wood, and carried the wood back to the cabin and dumped it beside the steps.

She could tell from the packed trail to the woodpile that Wade had been using his sled to move the wood. The sled would have been much more efficient, not to mention an easier way to move a quantity of wood, but the sled was now gone.

She carried armloads of wood until her arms quivered from the effort and she was so tired she wanted to puke.

The storm worsened. Wade had been right. The weather breeder had grown into a full-blown blizzard. The wind whistled through the spruce and fir trees and blew the snow sideways into her eyes. It blew so fiercely that it snatched the air from her lungs and rattled the cabin's storm windows, pressing against the log walls until they groaned in protest.

Faith removed the snowshoes and stuck them in the snowbank next to the steps, then began the laborious process of moving the wood she had just carried onto the porch where it wouldn't get covered by the blowing, drifting snow.

She reassured herself that the old cabin must have withstood many storms as intense as the one they were currently experiencing. She said a little prayer of thanks that she had resisted the urge to try to hike to Greenville. No living creature could survive this raging tempest without shelter.

Moving the wood up the steps sapped every reserve of energy she had. She still felt weakened from her near brush with freezing to death and soon had to sit on the steps and rest between loads.

She gave herself a twenty minute rest break and a cup of tea before she moved the wood from the porch to the woodbox. Her body felt so drained by then she staggered to the woodbox with the last armload of wood and sank to the floor in relief.

When she could move again she stood in the center of the cabin and did a slow pirouette. What else could they need over the next few days? A propane tank fed the gas stove for cooking and powered the well and water heater so no worries about losing power.

Now that her mind was functioning again she realized that of course a road led in to the cabin. She should have realized it when she took her shower. How else could a propane delivery be made?

A delivery truck meant that the cabin road led to a main road that would lead to a town. As long as she hiked the roads she could find her way back to Richard.

And none of that mattered at the moment. She had a deathly ill man on her hands.

Faith wondered where Wade kept the kerosene for the lanterns. She needed to ready a few candles in case it ran dry before she found the lantern fuel. Tomorrow she would look around the outside of the cabin, she decided. Wade had to have a storage place for large tools and flammables like the kerosene.

She quickly undressed inside the warm cabin, automatically hanging everything on the clothes rack by the wood stove to dry. She borrowed another of Wade's shirts and a pair of sweatpants, checked on the sick man and found him still burning hot with the fever.

"Don't you die on me, Wade Elliot. I want some answers from you."

She bathed him again with the cool water, then ate some of her cornbread with a bowl of soup before returning to her bedside chair with a book. She lit a lantern and turned it low to conserve fuel, just bright enough to read by if she held the book close to the flame.

Wade didn't look any better. If anything, he looked worse to her worried eyes. He moaned and thrashed, twisting the blankets around his hot, sweating body.

She set the book aside, and spoke to him in a soft voice, letting him know he wasn't alone. When he fell into a fitful sleep she took the opportunity to close her eyes and catnap.

Wade felt as if every cell in his body had been run beneath a pile driver and then set on fire. He tossed and turned, trying to escape the relentless pain and burning. Nothing he did eased his suffering.

He was finally reaping his reward, paying the price for causing his wife's death. This was what it felt like to burn in hell.

He pictured himself swimming in a cool lake but the water evaporated around his body, leaving him parched and still burning. A cool cloth gently wiped his brow and he grabbed the hand that held it.

"Susan!" Susan wasn't dead! Finding her battered, nearly lifeless body had been a nightmare of epic proportions. He needn't feel guilty that he had refused her a divorce when she told him that she no longer loved him.

The cool cloth left his body and he cried out, begging for its return. Susan's soft voice shushed him and the cloth came back and slowly wiped down his flaming chest and arms.

Wade felt tears squeeze out from under his clamped eyes. He tried to open them, to see Susan's fair head and blue eyes, but the light stabbed into his brain and he cried out with the pain.

What a selfish weakling he was. He grabbed Susan's wrist and refused to let her go. "Don't leave me," he begged.

"Shhhh. I'm not going anywhere," Susan replied. Only it wasn't Susan's light, breathy voice he heard. This woman's voice was throaty and buttery smooth, like warm maple syrup on a stack of sourdough pancakes.

Wade fought to open his eyes and glimpsed a halo of mahogany curls. Red flames sparked among the curls. Eyes the color of a tropical sea looked down on him with a tenderness that made his breath catch.

Where was he? Where was Susan?

He felt ice chips slip between his lips and he sucked on them greedily. The cold felt amazing against the inside of his cheeks. The ice melted and more were offered. He moaned with pleasure. His body was wiped down and when he began to shiver he felt the weight of blankets being piled on him. He slipped once more into the world of demons and nightmares.

"Susan!"

The shout woke Faith from a dream about Hope. In her dream, Hope was living in Faith's little house and systematically destroying everything that Faith possessed, an angelic smile on her face as she did.

Faith opened her eyes and looked at Wade. He was staring wide-eyed at Faith, his face flushed, his eyes still bright with fever and unfocused.

"Susan! You're not dead. I'm so sorry. I never got to tell you. I'm so sorry." He mumbled something that Faith couldn't make out.

"Shhhh. It's Faith, Wade. Susan isn't here. You're hallucinating from the fever." She filled the mug from a pitcher of water and held it to his lips with shaking hands. Wade's outburst frightened her. He was delirious and delirium wasn't good. It meant the fever still had the upper hand.

"Drink this. Here, swallow these two pills. You're still very ill."

"Susan. Don't blame me."

"Shhhh. I don't blame you. Rest now."

It took Faith several minutes to settle Wade down. She stood by the bed and stared at the sick man. Who was Susan? For that matter, who was Wade Elliot? She knew next to nothing about the man who had rescued her from certain death.

She ran a cool cloth gently over the puckered scar on Wade's right shoulder. She traced its round surface. Wade had another scar, similar but slightly larger, on the back side of the same shoulder. A bullet wound?

Faith turned and looked around the cabin. Somewhere in here there had to be a clue as to why a normal, healthy man would choose to hide away from society in a secluded cabin.

A chill ran down Faith's spine.

What if her first fear had been accurate? What if Wade Elliot was wanted by the law? What if he had murdered someone? Maybe he had killed Susan, whoever she was, and he didn't want her to blame him.

Or worse, what if he was a serial killer? Everyone interviewed after serial killers were caught always said how they couldn't believe that their nice, normal neighbor had turned out to be someone who enjoyed murdering people.

Faith began to pull books from the shelves, held each one upside down and riffled the pages. She worked methodically through each bookcase until she stood once more in front of the reference books.

She picked up the plumbing manual and flipped the pages. A folded piece of newspaper popped out and fell to the floor. She stared down at it, suddenly unsure.

Did she really want to know Wade's story? Wouldn't it be better if he told her himself? Was it even any of her business?

What if the newspaper article said he was a killer? She'd have to leave and bring back the authorities. She stared at the folded newsprint for several long moments, unsure what to do. Finally she set the plumbing manual down on the shelf and slowly picked up the piece of newsprint.

The first thing she noticed was the date: five years earlier. The headline screamed at her— WIFE OF BOSTON DETECTIVE SLAIN! Beneath the headline was a grainy photo of Wade Elliot, the expression on his face wild and terrible. Beside him two men were loading a gurney containing a body bag into an ambulance.

Faith sank to the floor and read the article, her hands shaking. When she finished there were tears running down her face. She brushed them away and carefully placed the article back inside the plumbing manual.

Wade Elliot was no killer. His wife had been beaten and killed by an unknown assailant. Wade had found her on their kitchen floor, barely alive. Despite the heroic efforts of the emergency responders, she had died within minutes of their arrival.

8

Outside the cabin, the blizzard raged for two days. Inside, Faith's existence narrowed down to tending the wood stove and tending the fevered Wade Elliot.

She moved between the wood pile, the woodbox, and the reading chair she had pulled beside the bed, with short forays to use the bathroom and the kitchen area for a cup of soup and cornbread.

On the third day she watched the sun break through the clouds from her seat beside the bed. The sky cleared to an indescribable deep blue, and everywhere the fresh snow sparkled so brilliantly that it was painful to behold.

Inside the cabin, Wade's fever worsened until he seemed to slip into a coma. Faith had begun to resign herself to losing Wade. She felt helpless and inadequate as she sat by, armed only with water and Tylenol, and tried to help him beat the fever that ravaged his body.

Wade's face had grown haggard and hollow, his eyes sunk deep into their sockets and bruised. He looked more dead than alive.

She found an old jar of vaseline in the bathroom and carefully spread it on his cracked and swollen lips with her finger. A small and futile gesture as far as his fever went, but it made her feel as if she was doing something to alleviate his suffering.

While she sat and watched over him she contemplated what she knew about Wade Elliot.

He had once been a homicide detective in Boston.

He had been married.

His wife had been brutally beaten to death.

Sometime after that event he moved to this isolated cabin in the Maine woods and took up carving.

He cared about people, otherwise he would not have saved Faith's life—but he didn't seem to need them. As far as she could see he lived in total isolation.

That was the sum total of what she knew about the man she had been living with for most of a week.

So little.

And yet she felt more comfortable in the one room cabin with the sick and fevered ex-cop than she had ever felt anywhere else.

She looked at the wasting body lying still as death. The fever still raged. The Tylenol and cool cloths had not helped to bring it down. Wade needed more. He needed to be immersed in an ice bath.

Faith frowned in speculation, then ran to the kitchen area and began to search the cupboards.

She found what she was looking for in the bottom drawer of the farthest set of cabinets. She grabbed the box of two gallon sized ziplock bags and raced out of the cabin with them.

The freshness of the outside world took Faith's breath away. The beauty of the quiet landscape, softened with its new coat of white powder, made her chest ache with something she couldn't name.

She drew the crisp and pure air deep into her lungs. It smelled of evergreen and freshness. A bluejay called to its friends, flashing its brilliant blue plumage as it swooped between trees on the edge of the clearing. The clear ra-ta-tat of a wood-pecker hammering a log sounded off to her right, hidden from her sight. The wildlife was getting back to their normal business after the storm.

Wade had chosen his place of healing well. She'd be damned if she was going to give up on him now.

She filled a half dozen bags with snow and carried them back inside, packing them alongside Wade's torso. She jammed two into his armpits and then sat back to watch over him. Whenever the bags half melted, she took them outside, dumped them and refilled them, over and over again, until finally the fever began to abate.

On the fifth day after Wade's fall through the ice he settled into a deep, calm sleep. Faith bathed his face and hands, covered him with the blankets, and went to stand on the porch and breath in the fresh air.

She wanted to throw open the windows and door to freshen the stale cabin but didn't dare. Not until Wade was strong enough to stand on his feet.

She pulled Wade's parka tighter around her body and stared at the pristine snow, unblemished by mankind other than her tracks to the woodpile. No gray from automobile exhaust, no footprints from unknown people scurrying to and fro. No unnatural piles of snow thrown high by snowplows. The landscape looked soft and undulating.

Cardinals sang in the evergreens, their bright red feathers lending a spot of color to the deep green and white landscape. A pair of crows floated silently across the bog, their sleek dark shapes reflecting the sun's rays. A red squirrel scolded her from the branches of an ancient maple.

She picked out the squirrel's round, black nest hole below the branch. Did Wade feed the squirrel? Is that why it scolded her? If she stayed here long enough she would get to know the animals who lived around the cabin.

Faith leaned against the porch rail and allowed the peace of nature to soak into her.

Today was to have been her wedding day. They had planned a small wedding, not even a wedding really, more of a short ceremony with a few witnesses. She wondered if Richard had called the Justice of the Peace to tell her the wedding had been postponed.

Hope was to have been one witness, Richard's friend Sam the other.

She squinted against the sunlight reflecting off the snow-covered bog. Was Richard out there right now looking for her? What story had Hope told him? What explanation had her sister given for her disappearance?

Richard knew Faith had spent the previous weekend snowmobiling and camping with Hope. She had called him the night before she had picked Hope up and told him about Hope's idea for a bridal shower for two.

What an idiot I am, thought Faith. Wade's right—a leopard doesn't change its spots.

The cabin door opened beside her. Wade stuck his head out, leaning heavily on the door jamb.

"Could you lend me a hand?" he rasped. "I desperately need a shower but I'm too weak to stand for more than a few minutes without help." As if to demonstrate, he sunk to his knees.

Faith sprang toward him with cry. "You idiot," she scolded. "You shouldn't be out of bed."

"I can't stand to be with myself," he answered with a grimace. "The bed needs to be changed and I smell worse than old gym socks. Don't argue, just help me."

Faith smiled. "It's so good to have you back, Mr. Elliot. I've missed your hard-assed personality. Yes, I will help you. Get back inside. If you catch another fever I may have to kill you myself."

Wade grinned at her and pulled himself to his feet. He stood swaying until Faith placed his arm over her shoulder and helped him to the table.

She tried to ignore his nakedness. After all, in the short time she had known Wade Elliot she had seen him naked more than clothed, she told herself.

Still, even in his weakened state, it was difficult not to notice his handsome and muscled masculinity. Faith's pulse kicked up.

"Wait here until I get undressed," she commanded, pulling out a dining chair and dumping him into it. She didn't want Wade to see how he affected her. "I can't go into the shower with you like this."

Wade's dimple appeared and his eyes shone with humor. "I'd never refuse a beautiful woman offering to undress and shower with me. How about some water while I wait?"

Faith smirked at him and gave him a mug of water. It pleased her that Wade had called her beautiful, even if he said it in jest. She wasn't used to being teased and found that she liked it. At least she liked Wade's teasing.

"I meant, wait while I take off your parka and my boots. I'm not getting naked in the shower with you, you dolt. I'm an engaged woman, remember? I'll just borrow some dry clothes when we're done."

"Pity," said Wade. "I'd hoped to get you naked again. I was too cold to appreciate it last time, and you were too cold for me to take advantage of it the first time. Third time's supposed to be a charm."

"You must be feeling better if you can think about sex. That's great news." Faith's face turned serious. "It was touch and go there for a while, Wade. I didn't know what to do and I felt helpless because I couldn't call anyone for help. If you had died I wouldn't even know who to contact."

Wade looked at her through heavy-lidded eyes.

Guilt tugged at him, but he refused to acknowledge it at the moment.

"Can I have my shower now, please?" he asked, changing the subject. He stood up and grabbed the table edge for support when his knees threatened to buckle beneath him. Damn, but he felt weak.

He hated having to ask for help from Faith but he had no choice. He was a man who believed in standing on his own two feet, and yet here he was, reduced to having a woman help him bathe.

They fumbled through the shower. Wade tried to support himself with one hand on the shower wall while Faith held him around the waist and he scrubbed ineffectively at the dried, sour sweat on his body.

"Let me," Faith said, seeing that Wade's weak attempt at washing wasn't working. She took the washcloth from him, soaped it up, and scrubbed his back.

Wade sighed with pleasure as Faith scrubbed the scum away and the hot water ran over him. He asked Faith to wash his hair for him, leaning against the shower stall with both hands, trapping her between them, and bowed his head before her.

With her chest in his face he couldn't help but notice how Faith's nipples puckered beneath her wet shirt.

He wanted to taste them, to tease them, but he

knew that she would leave the shower immediately if he tried and he didn't want that. She made him appreciate what it felt like to get close to a woman again.

He skipped the shave—his hands were too shaky. Faith offered to do it for him, but he declined after she admitted that she had never shaved a man's face before.

An hour later he sat in one of the chairs by the wood stove dressed in a clean pair of jeans and a long-sleeved tee sipping from a mug of soup. He ate slowly, aware that his belly had been given no food for several days. He didn't want it to cramp and reject the food.

Faith bustled about the cabin, setting it to rights. She pulled the other reading chair back to its place by the wood stove, stripped and remade the bed, and tossed the sheets into the washer. She hung the blankets and pillows outside on the porch rail to air and sanitize in the sun. She cleaned the bathroom and kitchen.

Wade watched her and realized that it felt nice to have a woman sharing the cabin with him. He caught Faith's hand as she walked by to hang his washed clothes on the drying rack.

"Thank you," he said simply.

Faith looked down at him, her eyes warm. "You're welcome. You'd have done the same for me. I'm just thankful you pulled through."

Wade kept hold of her hand. He took a drink

from the soup mug and chewed the vegetables thoroughly before swallowing.

"How long was I out of it?"

"Four full days. Today would have made five."

Wade beetled his dark eyebrows until a furrow appeared between them. "Five days. . . is today your wedding day?"

Faith pulled her hand away and nodded silently. She couldn't look Wade in the eyes. She turned away from him and busied herself hanging the wet laundry.

"I'm sorry," he said softly. "He should have come for you."

Faith's hands stilled, then resumed their work. "How could he?" she asked, forcing a light tone. "He has no idea where I am."

"I would've found you. I'd have tormented your sister until she told me where to find you. I wouldn't have left you to die."

Faith said nothing. Deep in her heart she agreed with Wade's words. If Richard truly loved her he'd have come searching for her. Strangely enough, she didn't feel as hurt as she expected to feel.

She finished hanging the wet clothes and sat in the other chair, stretching her stockinged feet toward the fire.

A comfortable silence stretched between them. Wade finished his soup and set the mug on the floor bedside the chair. He clasped his hands over his belly and allowed his eyes to close.

"Tell me about Susan."

The languid peace that Wade had been enjoying fled. His body tensed as it always did when he thought of his murdered wife. Guilt and rage leaped inside him at the mention of her name.

"How do you know about Susan?" His voice had lost all warmth and friendliness. It sounded cold and demanding. His cop voice. The one that said he would have answers—or else.

"You called out her name a few times while you were delirious. She must have been someone important to you. A woman you loved?"

Faith wasn't sure why she didn't simply tell Wade that she had found the newspaper story about Susan's murder. It felt important that he tell her himself, that he trust her enough to tell her about the event that had changed him from a homicide detective into a hermit woodcarver.

Wade sat back and closed his eyes. "She was my wife." His voice was flat, toneless.

Faith waited but he offered nothing more.

"Are you divorced?" she asked. It was obvious to her that Wade didn't want to talk about his dead wife, but she sensed that it was important for him to open up about Susan. There was more to Susan's story than what she had read in the article.

Something festered in Wade; she could feel it.

Something that needed to be excised if the man sitting beside her was to ever find real peace.

She waited patiently. Twenty minutes passed. Faith had come to the conclusion that Wade intended to say no more when he spoke again.

"No, I'm not divorced," he said. "I don't know if our marriage would've lasted—it isn't easy being a cops' wife, never knowing if I would live through another shift. But she was the one who ended up dying, not me. It should have been me, not her. She did nothing to deserve being beaten to death."

Faith felt the waves of tension coming off Wade's body. His clasped hands trembled slightly. She wondered if it was wrong to push him, but something told her that Wade had been holding this in, whatever "this" was, for far too long. Like the fever, it had to come out if he was going to heal.

"I'm so sorry," she said softly. "That must have been a terrible time for you. Did they catch your wife's killer?"

The familiar sense of helplessness rose inside Wade. He had worked his wife's murder harder than he had worked any other case, even though he had been warned to keep away from it. And like the lead detective on the case, he had made no headway.

Susan's killer had gotten away with beating his lovely wife and leaving her for Wade to find.

"No."

Faith waited. She sensed there was more to the story. That Wade had not yet shared the really terrible part. When he said nothing after several minutes she spoke again.

"Tell me. I know there's more, Wade."

Wade turned his head toward her, his eyes clouded with pain. He swallowed, tried to speak, swallowed again. He had never told anyone his terrible secret.

"She blamed me," he said. "She blamed me for her murder."

9

————

Faith stared at Wade. "How can that be possible? You didn't kill her did you?"

Wade scowled at her. "Of course not. I loved Susan." He hesitated, and then spoke so softly that Faith had to strain to hear him. "Her last words to me were, "blame you."

Faith's mouth fell open. "She told you that she blamed you? Are you sure that you heard her right? She actually spoke those two words?"

Wade pushed himself to his feet, forgetting how weak he was. He stumbled and grabbed the chair back for support. Damn, he hated feeling weak. He especially hated that somebody saw his weakness.

Just like that night he had found Susan—his pain and shock so sharp and raw that he couldn't hide it from the press. Well, he'd never let himself be put in that situation again.

His eyebrows came together in a scowl. Why did Faith have to bring up Susan? He didn't want to talk about Susan. He had found a small measure of peace living here in isolation and he didn't need some idiot woman who had plenty of her own issues to drag the painful past all up again.

"Wade?"

"Yes! I heard her say those words," he said through gritted teeth. "She could barely speak. It was a whisper, but I heard her. Now leave me alone."

He made his way across the room and fell onto the newly made bed, turning his back to Faith.

Faith had the good sense not to follow Wade and press him further. She picked up his soup mug and washed it, then settled back into her chair with a pencil and one of the blank sketch pads she had found in a drawer.

At home, in her real life, Faith wrote daily. It was how she managed to churn out a half-dozen novels a year—by sitting down for a minimum of four hours a day and putting words to paper. Of course she used a laptop instead of old-fashioned pen and paper, but the process was essentially the same.

She didn't consider writing a chore or a hardship. For her it was an escape from the empty life she had been forced to live. A way to deal with being unloved by anyone until Richard had come along.

Writing was a way to set her imagination and dreams free, to create worlds and relationships unlike her own, a world where women found their true loves and lived happily ever after.

She doodled on the upper edge of the page. Her heroes were usually strong, masculine men whose love was equally strong and true. Why was it that after hearing Wade's story, Richard's love suddenly felt inadequate, almost one-dimensional in contrast?

Faith shook off the treacherous thought. Perhaps she expected too much from love.

Perhaps she expected too much from Richard. Richard *had* told her that he loved her when he had asked her to marry him. At the time Faith had thought that hearing a man's declaration of love would fill her with heat and passion and tenderness.

She could admit now that that hadn't happened with Richard. She had looked at him with considering eyes and accepted his marriage proposal because she knew in her heart that she would never receive another.

She recalled the feel of Richard's lips on hers after she had agreed to marry him. Thin, dry, and cold. Not warm and demanding the way she knew

Wade's kisses would be. She had felt nothing at Richard's touch. It had been like kissing a brother.

Faith tapped the pencil on the sketch pad. She had accepted Richard's marriage proposal and she would do as she promised. Not everyone was lucky enough to find a relationship filled with passion. With love that filled the soul.

A tear dropped onto the pad and she brushed it away. Until this moment she hadn't realized how desperately she had wanted Richard to come for her, to prove that he needed her and loved her enough to go out of his comfort zone to find her and rescue her.

Was that why Hope had abandoned her? To prove to Faith that Richard was no different from anyone else in her life? To show Faith that he didn't really love her?

She remembered Wade's quiet words at the table when he had told her that he would search for the woman he loved. In her heart, Faith knew that Wade wouldn't let anything short of death keep him from his woman.

He was like the heroes in her novels—stout-hearted and willing to give their lives to protect those they loved.

Faith brushed another tear from her cheek before it could fall. She was being foolish. Her heroes were make-believe men, men who didn't exist in the real world, or if they did, they were few and far between. They were certainly not meant for an unlovable woman like herself.

She wished she had a close girlfriend to talk with, someone with more experience, someone who could tell Faith how it should be between a man and a woman when they loved one another.

Yes, she wrote romance, but how realistic were her stories? She made them up from her own dreams and a steady diet of reading other romance writers to help her with writing the physical side of the relationships.

The sad truth was, she had no business writing romance. She had barely been kissed and it had been a disappointing experience. What did she know about love and passion?

Faith turned her head and stared at Wade's sleeping form. His breathing was deep and smooth, a sure sign that he was indeed on the mend. She took in his broad shoulders, the way they tapered down to his hips and long, powerful legs.

The sudden, overwhelming urge to crawl into the bed and cuddle against Wade's back surprised her. She suppressed it and forced herself to think about his murdered wife.

She found it hard to believe that Susan had blamed him for her murder. She suspected that Wade had misheard Susan's last words, that the guilt over the fact that he hadn't been there to protect his wife had colored the words he had thought he heard.

Blame you. What had Susan been trying to say? Faith shook her head. How would she know? She had never met Wade's wife and had no clue how the dead woman's mind worked.

She pushed thoughts of Wade and his murdered wife from her own mind and began work on her newest novel. It was her favorite plot line yet, about a manly man who rescues a woman from certain death in the frozen north.

Over the next few days, Faith and Wade settled into a relaxed daily routine. Faith had resigned herself to waiting until spring to hike to Greenville. Her hope that Richard would come to find her faded a little more with each passing day until it disappeared altogether.

What surprised her the most however, was that her desire to leave the peaceful cabin had also faded.

Wade rapidly regained his strength. An easy friendship began to grow between them. Neither of them brought up Susan's murder or Richard's failure to find Faith. Faith spent the days writing while Wade worked on a new carving.

In the evenings after dinner they sat beside the

wood stove and talked, or played cards or backgammon. Spending time with someone other than Hope was a novel experience for Faith.

Something that she finally identified as happiness began to sprout and grow inside her. She felt lighter and freer. She felt as if she was becoming a different, better Faith.

Faith refused Wade's nightly offer to share his bed and slept on the floor by the wood stove instead. Her desire to sleep with Wade grew with each passing day, and for that reason she knew she couldn't.

Although she had missed the wedding, she still considered herself an engaged woman. She had promised herself to another, and even though she could see that Richard wasn't half the man that Wade Elliot was, she would keep her promise.

Unfortunately being with Wade created feelings and sensations in Faith that she had never before experienced. Sensations that grew harder to ignore the more time she spent in his company. The harder they grew to ignore, the harder she fought to ignore them.

Once, during dinner, they had both reached for the salt shaker at the same time. Wade's fingers had brushed the back of Faith's hand. They had both frozen, and then Wade had gently stroked the back of Faith's hand with two fingers. She had mumbled something inane and jerked her hand away.

Another time she had caught him watching her with a strange heat in his eyes, a heat that made her insides feel all warm and soft and trembly.

Oh yes, it was getting harder and harder to deny that she was strongly attracted to Wade Elliot.

She had never told Richard that she was still a virgin. Conversation about their sexual histories had never come up between them. She could experience sex with Wade and Richard would never know.

But in her heart, Faith knew that if she allowed Wade to make love to her she would never be able to give herself to another man. Once Wade marked her as his it would be forever.

She couldn't think of anything she'd like more.

That knowledge frightened her and saddened her. Wade was an emotionally damaged man. Faith didn't know if he'd ever be capable of loving another woman after the brutal loss of his first wife. After the accidental touch over the salt shaker she took great care to keep her distance from him.

One morning, nearly two weeks after her missed wedding, Faith heard a small plane engine. Wade was in the shower. She grabbed his parka and went outside to search the skies for the plane.

It appeared far down the bog, a mere glint of

sunlight in a cobalt blue sky flying straight at the cabin. As it drew closer she made out its bright red wings and body. The plane flew low and slowly up the center of the bog, dropped a package onto the snow, and banked up over the trees surrounding the cabin. A moment later it circled and headed back down the bog with a waggle of its wings.

"Wade! Wade!" Faith rushed back into the cabin. "A plane was just here. It dropped something onto the bog. I'm going to go get it."

Faith grabbed her balaclava and mittens and strapped on the snowshoes, then made her way down the hillside and onto the bog. The package had a small red parachute attached to it, making it easy to see in the snow.

When she arrived at the package she saw that it was a good-sized box that had several wrappings of strapping tape around it. She flipped it over. "Cuz" was written in heavy black marker.

She lifted the package, intending to carry it back to the cabin, but was out of breath after only a dozen or so steps. They needed the sled to haul it back with.

Once his strength had returned Wade had tried to retrieve the sled, carefully skirting the thin ice around it. But the sled was frozen solid beneath new ice with no way to get it out without risking another plunge into the bog. It would have to wait for retrieval until the spring thaw.

Faith set the box down and made her way back to the cabin. Wade stood waiting for her on the front porch, his dark hair still wet from his shower. His eyes held an amused expression.

"I see Rafe has been by," he said with a smile.

Faith stopped at the bottom of the steps, momentarily arrested by the dimple in Wade's cheek. She longed to trace it with her finger and plant a kiss near it.

"Faith?"

Faith tore her eyes away from Wade's face and blushed.

"Who is Rafe?" she asked, leaning down and busying herself with the snowshoes to hide her embarrassment.

"My cousin, Raphael Winehurst. He owns a small charter plane service in Greenville. He drops me care packages every month during the winter. Says he feels sorry for me, but I know his wife makes him do it. Sarah is a nurturer. She's made it her mission in life to take care of lost souls and considers me to be her most important project."

Faith filed away the information. Someday she'd like to talk with Sarah Winehurst about Wade.

"How can we get the box to the cabin without the sled? I tried to carry it but it's too awkward and heavy."

"Guess we'll have to come up with a makeshift sled. Let me get dressed and grab the key for the storage area." Wade disappeared inside the cabin and returned a few minutes later dressed in a heavy wool sweater and down vest.

Wade grabbed the shovel from the porch and shoveled a narrow path in the snow at the base of the porch around the side of the cabin where the woodpile sat. The area beneath the porch had been closed in at some point in the past. Faith noticed a padlock hanging from a stainless hasp in the center of two hinged doors.

Wade shoveled a clear space and pulled a key from his pocket. He unlocked the padlock and pulled open the left section of the wall.

"Clever to use the space under the porch for storage," Faith said as she snapped on the flashlight Wade had handed her. "Your idea?"

"Nope. This cabin has been in the family for four generations. I think my grandfather closed this in. Shine that light over here."

Faith played the light quickly over the interior. Adirondack chairs sat stacked and covered with deflated inner tubes and large clay flower pots. A kayak hung above her head from the porch's support joists. A canoe hung beside it. Garden tools and step ladders and all the detritus one usually stored in a cellar or garage filled the space.

Wade stepped inside the dark space with Faith close on his heels. He stopped abruptly and she bumped into his back. He turned and grasped her shoulders.

"You all right?"

"Yes." She was standing very close to Wade, close enough to smell his shampoo and soap. His hands tightened on her shoulders. She swayed slightly, bringing her body even closer to his.

Faith's pulse rate kicked up. She couldn't pull herself away. She knew she should, but she couldn't find the strength. In fact, she wanted to get even closer. Her body felt hot and achy, not in a sickness kind of way, but in a way she'd never experienced before.

She lifted her chin slightly and looked into Wade's face. The deep shadows of the enclosure made the planes of his face look more severe than usual, almost predatory, she thought. He was watching her closely through half-lidded eyes. She saw his gaze drop to her lips and she unconsciously licked them.

Wade let out a muffled groan and slid one arm around Faith. He grasped the back of her head with his free hand as he pulled her against him. He gently kissed her temple, then her cheek, then the corner of her mouth.

Faith's lips parted and her breath came in short gasps. Her arms still at her sides, she turned her face slightly and pressed her lips to Wade's.

"Faith." Wade tightened his grip on her and

sought to separate her lips with his tongue. She pressed her lips together.

Unbelievable, he thought with surprise. This beautiful, intelligent, creature lacks even the most basic experience of kissing. How could her fiancé not want to kiss that sexy mouth?

"No, sweetheart," he whispered. "Open your mouth. Let me taste you."

Hesitantly, unsure she was doing it correctly, Faith parted her lips slightly. Wade ran the tip of his tongue gently over her bottom lip and then pushed into her mouth and sought her tongue with his. She sucked on him and he groaned.

Faith pulled her head away in alarm. "What is it? Did I hurt you?"

Wade pulled her head to his shoulder and chuckled in her ear. He pressed his lips to her hair, then gently bit her earlobe.

"God no," he rasped. "It's just been so long, and you taste and feel amazing. You're doing everything right, sweetheart."

He adjusted her head and pressed his lips to hers again, slowly and gently, and this time he was rewarded with the shy touch of her tongue.

"Yes, Faith. Taste me," he said against her mouth. He held himself back while she explored, tentatively at first, then with more confidence.

He sucked gently on her tongue and was rewarded with a soft groan. Her arms crept up and circled his neck.

Filled with an agonizing need, Wade pulled of his gloves and pushed his hands inside the open parka and under the shirt she wore. He caressed Faith's smooth, muscled back and reached inside her pants to cup her bottom. She trembled under his hands and he lost his self-control.

He pulled her against his throbbing erection, wanting her to know how much he desired her. He wanted her naked, wanted her beneath him, open to his explorations. He wanted to taste all of her, wanted to fill her—

"Wade! Wade! Stop!" she said against his mouth.

Belatedly Wade realized that Faith was pushing against his chest with both hands, trying to break his hold on her. He released her immediately, kicking himself mentally for behaving like a randy teen-aged boy. What an old fool he was. He had pushed innocent Faith too hard, too fast.

He took a few ragged breaths, fighting to dampen his lust.

"Sorry. I pushed you too fast," he said, his voice gruff.

Faith blinked back tears and gave a small smile. "No, it's all right." Her voice sounded weak and shaky. Her body still ached and trembled from Wade's touch. She longed to experience whatever happened next, but she couldn't. She took a deep, calming breath.

"I-I got caught up. This wasn't your fault. I wanted you to kiss me, Wade. But I can't lead you on. I'm engaged to be married and what we were doing wasn't right and proper. It was all my fault. I'm sorry."

Wade scowled. "You're engaged to marry a man who didn't care enough to come looking for you."

A look of sadness and resignation came into Faith's eyes. She leaned down to pick up the dropped flashlight and handed it to him.

"That may be, but I promised. I'll wait outside for you to find what you're looking for."

10

FAITH STOOD outside the storage enclosure while she waited for Wade, still trembling from the recent experience. She felt a little dizzy and otherworldly. Her lips tingled in a pleasant way.

If one of Wade's kisses could elicit this level of response from her, she couldn't imagine what she would feel with her naked body pressed against his.

She shuddered and tried to push the image of Wade's naked flesh from her thoughts. Tension throbbed in her lower body. The feel of Wade's erection, so hard and masculine, had startled her. None of the romance novels she read had prepared her for the magnificent, utter virility, of Wade's body.

An embarrassed flush crept up her neck. What an arrogant fool she'd been, writing pretend sex scenes with no experience of her own to draw upon. She could only guess that her readership must have equally non-existent or dismal sex lives of their own or they wouldn't continue to buy her books.

Well, she could at least do a better job with her kissing scenes from now on. She pulled off her mitten and touched her fingers to her tingling lips.

Under the porch, Wade stood for moment while he got his ragged breathing under control. The kiss had surprised him—not because it was unexpected—he had been thinking about kissing Faith almost since the day she'd been walking around the cabin dressed in nothing but his quilt.

No, what had surprised him was the intensity of his desire for her. He wanted to devour her, to explore every inch of her lovely, athletic body. Her kiss had left him feeling shaky, a reaction he had never experienced before.

With Susan, Wade had always been careful of her delicateness. He had been afraid of hurting her physically; consequently he had always held himself back, never fully letting himself go. Never feeling that he could.

He had loved his wife, but there had been barriers between them that he had never fully understood.

In that moment, Wade realized that he should have agreed to Susan's request for a divorce. She had been smarter about their marriage than he had. She had known that they weren't a good fit, despite the fact that they were high school sweethearts as well as good friends.

The kiss with Faith had shown Wade that there were women in the world who were capable of a passion equal to any man's. Equal to his.

Unfortunately this woman, the woman he wanted to explore this discovery with, was promised to another man.

Ah well, he'd live. He knew how to control himself. After all, he'd done it with Susan for over twelve years. His wife had never been crazy about sex. It had been the most obvious area in their marriage where they'd been incompatible.

For the first time in his life, Wade could admit that his marriage had not been ideal. He shook his head in bemusement. All it had taken was one taste of Faith's lips and mouth. He wondered what it would feel like to possess Faith's body.

"Don't go there, boyo," he muttered to himself as he felt his body stir again. He pushed aside thoughts of sex with Faith and concentrated on the task at hand.

"You okay?" Wade asked as he came out of the storage area with a long toboggan under his arm. His expression showed concern, but his eyes crinkled at the outer corners with humor.

Faith frowned at him indignantly. "Of course I'm okay. It was just a kiss."

Wade's grin widened. "Speak for yourself, sweetheart. That was the best kiss I've had in a long, long time. Maybe even ever."

Faith blushed with pleasure. She looked for a way to change the subject and spied the toboggan. "I'll take that while you get the padlock."

Wade handed her the toboggan. "I'll be right back." He disappeared into the enclosure, emerging a minute later with a pair of old-fashioned wood and leather snowshoes.

"I didn't realize these were still here," he said, sticking them into the snow while he reset the padlock. "I thought Rafe had taken them home with him last winter but I was wrong."

He looked at Faith. She was glaring at him.

Wade held up a palm. "Honest, Faith. I didn't know these were here. But now that we have two sets of shoes, what do you say we go get Rafe's package together?"

Faith wanted to be mad at Wade for the snowshoes, but she couldn't seem to muster any real anger. He had made an honest mistake, she told herself.

Besides, if she had left when she intended, she would have been stuck in the blizzard and probably wouldn't have survived. And Wade certainly would've died after his fall into the bog.

"These are nice shoes," he remarked. "I think they were my uncle's, then Rafe's, then Rafe lent them to me until I bought the new ones. They're much better shoes than the aluminum-framed ones I use now. I think I'll go back to these," he added to himself.

A mantle of sadness settled over Faith, dulling the bright day.

Once she was gone.

Wade hadn't said the words, but the unspoken thought hung in the air between them.

"Give me those." She took the snowshoes and left Wade with the toboggan.

Standing at the foot of the steps, feeling confused by her feelings, Faith watched Wade clean and wax the toboggan's bottom.

Why did she feel sad at the thought of leaving? She wanted to get back to her life, didn't she?

"You ready?"

She forced herself to smile at Wade. "Let's go see what your cousin sent you."

Faith bent down to put on the snowshoes.

"Give me those," he said, with his hand out. He took the shoes from Faith and bungeed the two sets onto the back of the toboggan.

"What are you doing? We need those."

A boyish grin broke out on Wade's face. "Not yet we don't. We're going for a ride first." He sat in front of the snowshoes and spread his thighs. "Sit here, in front of me and grab my legs."

Faith hesitated, but her curiosity won out. She sat between Wade's legs and grabbed his thighs. He trapped her body between his legs and pressed his feet onto the curved front of the toboggan. His arms went around her as he grabbed onto the toboggan's rope.

Wade pushed off and the toboggan began to move slowly toward the bog, picking up speed as it slid down the hillside.

"Hang on tight," Wade said into Faith's ear. She leaned back, feeling safe and excited with his chest pressed firmly into her back and his thighs and arms boxing her in.

They were flying down the hill now, snow spraying out the sides of the toboggan like water from a boat's prow. She screamed and laughed aloud with excitement. She felt as if the toboggan could become airborne at any second. Never in her life had she done anything for the sheer fun of it.

The toboggan rocketed out onto the bog and kept going, eventually slowing and coming to a stop.

"That was fantastic!" Faith said, laughing. "Can we do it again?" She twisted her head to look at Wade.

Wade grinned down at her sparkling eyes and planted a quick kiss on her nose. "If you wish, m'lady. But first we have to hike back. That's always the down side of sledding. One has to work for the few moments of excitement."

"I don't mind," Faith said as she scrambled to her feet. "That was awesome. I've never sledded before. It felt incredible, like we were flying."

Wade looked up at Faith in disbelief. "Honestly? You've never gone sledding? What kind of childhood did you have, anyway? Every kid in Maine goes sledding in the winter. It's what we do."

As soon as the teasing words were out of his mouth he wished he could snatch them back. The sparkle left Faith's eyes and shadows filled them again.

"Never mind," he said, getting to his feet. "We can toboggan all day long if you like, to make up for your sad lack of fun as a child. And tomorrow too. And the day after, until you get so sick of it you'll wish I'd never started this."

He handed Faith her snowshoes and was rewarded with a smile. Another small chunk of the ice block that insulated his heart melted away. He had forgotten how good giving another human being pleasure could feel.

They hauled the carton back to the cabin and set it on the porch, then made several more runs with the toboggan. With each successive run the track became smoother and faster and the toboggan carried them farther and farther onto the bog. After the fourth run Faith's legs wobbled and she was forced to admit that she couldn't manage the hike back to the cabin, so Wade made her stay on the toboggan and he hauled her home.

They shared lunch and settled in front of the fire with Rafe's care package. Faith watched as Wade expertly slit it open with his pocketknife.

"What sort of stuff does your cousin send you?" she asked.

Wade shrugged. "Food mostly, recent newspapers, razor blades. Stuff like that. I have a couple magazine subscriptions that go to his house. I have a standing order for certain things that I need and he or Sarah usually add a few surprises."

He reached into the box and pulled out canned items: peaches, tuna, tomatoes. Dried beans and pasta followed. He pulled a smaller box from the large carton and smiled.

Wade carefully slit open the box and pulled out an object wrapped in bubble-wrap and taped. He removed the bubble-wrap and revealed three egg cartons. Opening the top one, he grinned at Faith and held it out for her inspection.

"You wouldn't believe the mess Rafe's first few tries made. He's got it figured out now. Everything else survives the drop pretty well, but the eggs stymied him for a long time. I hate freeze-dried eggs so I challenged him to find a way to get me fresh ones. Rafe never could resist a challenge. We'll have omelets for dinner."

Wade set down the eggs and pulled a pile of newspapers and magazines from the bottom of the carton.

"I'll put the food away. Would you like a cup of tea while we catch up on the outside world?"

Faith helped Wade with the foodstuffs and they both settled into the reading chairs with the sections of the papers that interested them. All was peaceful and quiet for an hour.

Faith shot a sideways glance at Wade. Sitting with him in front of the wood stove with mugs of hot tea and reading the papers made her feel happy and wistful at the same time. This was something she desperately wanted, to have a relationship where the man she loved could sit with her just like this and feel content.

There were no head games with Wade, she realized. She didn't feel as if she had to be on her guard with him. True, he hadn't let her leave when she'd wanted, but he had been right to keep her here. She would have perished in the storm for sure.

She felt content. She considered what that meant. The truth was she could be happy living here with Wade Elliot. She had grown to love the big, complicated man in the short time they had known one another.

Too bad he still carried a torch for his dead

wife, she reminded herself. Besides, she was still engaged to marry Richard.

She tried to picture Richard sitting next to the wood stove quietly reading with her, or sledding, and couldn't. Richard didn't do things because they were fun.

Faith pushed the unwelcome thoughts away and returned to her reading. Rafe had included the Bangor Daily News and Portland Press Herald Sunday papers. She read the world news, then the local news, then picked up the society/people section.

She couldn't believe how little she had thought about the real world happenings since she had been stuck in Wade's cabin. She had missed the annual flower and garden show that had taken place last weekend in Portland. She always enjoyed going to the flower show, loved the fresh smells and colors of the flowers during the dreary part of winter.

She flipped the page and idly ran her eyes over the wedding page, stopping at a familiar name. The names took a moment to sink in.

Faith's hands began to shake. A low moan escaped her throat. She dropped the paper.

"Faith? What's wrong?" Wade jumped to his feet and came to her side. "Tell me." He put his hand on her shoulder and squeezed gently. "Are you ill?"

Dammit, he should've known better than to let

her make so many toboggan runs down the hill. She'd had a rough time of it between her own hypothermia and then nursing him through his fever.

Faith shook her head. "I'm not ill." Her voice sounded weak and shaky to her ears. She cleared her throat and tried to speak more clearly.

"I just—I just read an unexpected wedding announcement." Faith waited for the piercing pain that usually followed one of Hope's betrayals, but this time she felt only a cold numbness. And underneath the cold, maybe a tiny kernel of relief.

Wade's eyes were puzzled. "Someone you know?" When Faith looked up at him the shock in her eyes made him want to pull her onto his lap and rock her like a young child.

Without thinking, he nudged her aside and sat in her chair, then pulled her onto his lap.

She didn't fight him. She curled into his chest, seeking his warmth and comfort.

"You could say that," she answered, her head against his chest. "Richard married my sister Hope last Sunday. She even wore my dress."

11

———————

"AW HELL. I'm sorry, Faith. All I can say is the man didn't deserve you."

Wade reached down and picked the wedding announcement off the floor. The grainy black and white photo showed a bride and groom smiling brightly at the camera. He peered closely at Hope Donahue. She looked a lot like Faith, but with blonde hair and a straight nose. He couldn't tell Hope's eye color from a black and white image, but he was willing to bet that they weren't as exotic and mesmerizing as her sister Faith's turquoise eyes.

The groom looked like a loser, Wade thought with satisfaction. Tall and slim to the point of skinny, with wire-framed glasses and a weak chin,

Richard Trask looked like a pasty-faced scholar who spent all his time sitting inside dusty libraries.

"Looks like Richard didn't want to waste all the arrangements I made," Faith observed dryly, her voice stronger. "I wonder if they're headed to Savannah for their honeymoon? Richard had some research he wanted to do there so he talked me into a working honeymoon."

She waited for Wade to read the announcement and tell her how Hope looked like an angel, and what a fool Faith had been to believe that any man wanted to marry her over Hope.

"You're prettier than your sister. And obviously the groom is a huge loser," Wade said. "First of all, how could he marry someone else if there was a chance you were still alive? And second, what red-blooded man would want to think about work when he could have you in his bed to make love to? If you ask me, you're lucky your sister took Richard off your hands."

Faith blinked. She lifted her head from Wade's chest and scowled at him. "Are you blind? Hope is beautiful. She looks like an angel. Everyone says so. Can't you see that?"

She snatched the paper from Wade's hand and looked at the announcement again. Maybe the photographer had taken a bad picture of Hope. But no, she knew that couldn't be. Somehow Hope never allowed a bad photo to be taken of herself.

Faith studied the photo, trying to see how Wade had missed the truth. There was Hope with her perfect hair and perfect make-up and her perfect straight nose. Faith reached up and absently rubbed the bump in her own nose.

Hope looked fabulous in the bronze silk sheath that Faith had chosen for her wedding dress, she observed ruefully. Her sister must have let herself into Faith's house and taken the dress. To her surprise, Faith felt more anger over the loss of the dress than she did over losing Richard.

"She looks . . . shallow and conceited," Wade said, looking down at the paper in Faith's hand. "She looks like the world owes her. She reminds me of a package that's bright and shiny on the outside and empty on the inside. Or worse, since I know a little about your sister, she's like biting into a perfect looking apple and finding a worm and a big rotten spot inside."

Faith's mouth dropped open. Then she closed it and giggled. She dropped the paper on the floor and wrapped her arms around Wade's body.

"Thank you," she whispered against his neck. "You're the first person who's ever taken my side over Hope's."

Wade pulled Faith tighter against him.

"I've only known you a short while, Faith Donahue, but I know enough to recognize that you are a special woman. Most women would have gone into hysterics if they had found themselves abandoned in the northern Maine woods in winter time, but you were strong enough to try to make your way to safety."

"I didn't have much of a choice," murmured Faith. "I wasn't ready to die." She snuggled against Wade's chest. He felt strong and warm and comforting and she loved being held on his lap like a child.

"Don't sell yourself short. You had two choices: live or die. You chose to live, which was the tougher choice. I've never met another woman who would have attempted to hike out of the mountains like you did. That took a lot of guts. Most women would've sat in the tent and prayed that someone would show up to rescue them. "

Faith thought about Wade's comment. She had been selling herself short all her life, she realized. Always measuring herself against Hope.

Hope, who was loved more by their mother.

Hope, who made friends more easily and always had dates while Faith had none because she'd been too shy and insecure to accept a date.

Hope, who was everything that Faith was not.

She couldn't blame it all on Hope, she saw that now. She had allowed her sister to beat her down. She had taken Hope's criticisms as truths and internalized them until they became true. What a weak fool she had been.

"Faith?" Wade tilted her chin up with one hand and looked into her face.

Their mouths were only inches apart. She felt his warm breath fall upon her cheek and reached up to stroke his jaw with her fingers. "Kiss me," she whispered. "Please."

"Gladly," answered Wade as he lowered his lips to hers. He kissed her gently, long and slow and lingering. Kissed her lips and chin and nose, cheeks and temple, then back to her mouth again.

Faith made a small moan in her throat and he cupped the back of her head and tilted it until he could kiss the length of her smooth throat and the sensitive spot beneath her ear. He bit her earlobe gently and returned once more to her mouth.

Faith broke off the kiss. "Wade—" she hesitated. "No one has ever kissed me like this before. It feels . . . it feels so good," she whispered.

Wade chuckled and smiled against her mouth. "Don't sound so surprised. Wait until you see what else I can do for you." He stood up with Faith in his arms.

Faith squealed and pressed her face into Wade's neck. "You can't carry me—I'm too tall, too-too-too big and heavy. What are you doing?"

Wade looked at the woman in his arms. His eyebrows beetled together in a frown. How could such a beautiful, intelligent woman have serious self-image issues? Well, he would make it his goal to change them for the better. And he'd start now.

He kissed the top of her head. "You aren't too big, sweetheart. You're perfect as far as I can tell. As for what I'm doing—what I intend to do to you requires someplace more comfortable than a chair —at least for the first time," he answered, his voice gruff but amused.

Faith swallowed. She knew what Wade intended: knew, and at the same time didn't know. This was all uncharted territory for her. She had never felt this excited and nervous before.

"Okay," she answered, her voice muffled against his neck.

He smelled so good. She'd be happy doing nothing but this, she thought—being held in Wade's strong arms with her nose buried against him, smelling his clean, masculine scent.

Wade stopped beside the bed and carefully laid Faith on top of the blankets. The cabin was plenty warm enough to get naked outside of the covers. He wanted to see all of Faith. He didn't want her hiding under the blankets.

He knew she had no sexual experience. That was all right with him. In fact, it pleased him to know that he was going to be the man to introduce Faith to the pleasures of the bedroom. He was going to make damned sure that her first time was as exciting and pleasurable as he could possibly make it.

"You're so beautiful," he said, looking down at her.

Faith shook her head. "No, I'm not. Hope—"

Wade placed a finger against her lips. He looked steadily into her eyes. "*You are beautiful*, Faith. Trust me."

He leaned down and unbuttoned her shirt and spread the two sides, exposing her naked breasts.

Faith blushed and brought her arms up to cover herself.

"No, don't hide from me."

Wade lay down beside her on the bed He slid one arm under her neck and pulled her close against his body, running his free hand slowly up and down her back beneath the shirt. He repeated the long, smooth strokes over and over, down her naked back to her bottom, and back up to her shoulders, until he felt Faith relax against him.

He kissed her mouth gently, then firmer, working his way inside, retreating, going back for more, teasing her until he felt her tongue reach out to taste him.

He continued to stroke her back while he kissed her, waiting for her to show him she that was ready for more.

He was in no hurry. Early on with Susan he had

been in a fumbling hurry, too young and inexperienced to realize that a woman needed time to warm up and get used to the differentness of the male body.

Today, even though he had not lain with a woman for over five years, he wanted to savor every moment of the experience. More than that, he wanted to make Faith's first time an unforgettable and pleasant experience.

He moved his kisses to below her ear and down the smooth column of her slender neck, worked his way slowly down over her shoulders to her breasts where he licked and suckled until Faith squirmed and moaned.

Wade slid his thumbs into her long underwear and pulled them off her body in one smooth motion, tossing them to the floor beside the bed. Again Faith tried to cover herself.

"No." He looked down at the deep red triangle of curls that covered her most secret place. "You have nothing to hide from me. You are a beautiful creature, Faith. Let me look at you."

"I-I'm not sure what to do." The heat in Wade's eyes as he looked at her naked body made Faith feel strangely warm and womanly; both sensations excited her while being alien to her.

"You don't have to do anything at the moment. Let me make love to you and we'll learn what you like together."

"But what about you? This isn't fair. I should be doing something for you."

"Shhh," Wade said as he moved down her body and began to run his tongue around her navel, dipping lower, then returning to her mouth for long, slow kisses until he felt her relax again.

"Don't worry, I'll get my turn," he murmured against her abdomen.

Faith let Wade explore and taste every part of her body until the heat and tension inside her had built to an intolerable pitch.

"Wade?" She panted and arched against him. He was doing unimaginable things to her with his mouth and fingers and the pressure continued to mount inside her until she thought she would burst open. She wanted something, her body demanded it, but she didn't know what or how to get there.

Wade lifted his head. His dark hair and blue eyes gleamed in the soft light of the wood fire. "Yes?" He gave a low laugh and flicked the tip of his tongue over her most sensitive spot. "Do you want me to stop?"

Faith could only moan in response. She reached down and threaded her fingers through his hair, holding him to her. The tension in her body grew unbearable. "Yes. No! I need, I need . . ."

Wade took her into his mouth and sucked and teased while gently thrusting two fingers inside her. Suddenly the tension released. She cried out as her body shattered with pulsing spasms that left her feeling limp and wrung-out.

She took a deep, shuddering breath. "Oh my god."

Wade stood beside the bed and looked down at Faith with a smug smile. "There are plenty more where that came from."

He pulled off his tee shirt, undid his pants, and stepped out of them before climbing back onto the bed beside Faith. She looked at him shyly.

"Will you teach me how to please you?" she asked.

"Gladly. I'll be right back." Wade slipped off the bed and went into the bathroom. He rummaged under the sink cabinet for the box of condoms his cousin Rafe had placed there when Wade first moved into the cabin.

At the time Wade had barely acknowledged Rafe's optimism with a dismissive head shake and promptly forgot about the condoms. He'd had no use for them until today. He wasn't even sure they were still there.

He found the box of condoms in the far back corner of the cabinet and sent up a silent thank you to his cousin. He brought the whole box back to the bed and placed it in the bedside table.

Faith turned out to be a quick and enthusiastic learner. Now that she knew first hand how incredible sex could feel, she wanted to elicit the same responses in Wade.

He was a patient teacher, demanding that she experience several more orgasms while she learned his body, until the moment came when he couldn't bear it any longer.

He showed her how to dress him with a condom and placed himself between Faith's thighs where he gently probed, withdrew, thrust deeper, and repeated until she begged him to fill her. That was all the encouragement Wade needed. He held her and buried himself inside her.

Faith dug her fingers into Wade's shoulders and moaned.

"You feel so good," she said, gently nipping at his chest. "This feels so good."

Wade picked up the pace until they were both panting. He waited for Faith to explode one last time, and then let himself go with a triumphant cry. He collapsed on top of her and waited for his pulse rate to slow.

Faith stroked Wade's back. Her body felt lush, replete, and very, very content. Sex with Wade was far better than any sex scene she had ever read or imagined.

They dozed off together and woke ravenously hungry.

12

―――――

"You get the fire, I'll cook," said Faith when they were ready to leave the bed. She picked the borrowed shirt off the floor, put it on, and padded barefoot to the kitchen area without bothering with her pants.

Interesting how sex can erase all sense of modesty, she thought. She would have to remember to include the sensation in her current novel. In fact, maybe she'd describe her recent experience with Wade in detail. It was better than any seduction scene she had ever read.

The thought made warmth pool in her lower body and she smiled.

"What are you smiling about?" Wade asked from near the stove.

He hadn't bothered with a shirt and Faith

found her eyes drawn to the gleaming mat of dark hair that covered Wade's chest and drew her eyes down the narrowing path of hair until it disappeared beneath the waistband of his low-slung jeans.

She gave him a wide smile. "I was thinking that now I can write sex scenes and actually have a clue as to what I'm writing about."

Wade stopped and stared at her, the stove lid open and the log in his hand momentarily forgotten.

"How does a virgin write sex scenes?"

"With very little detail, I assure you. I mostly allude to the sex and focus on other aspects of the relationship instead."

"Are you a published author?"

Faith nodded. "Yep. I have a pretty good following. I try to give my readers a new romance every six-to-eight weeks, but I've been having a little trouble coming up with new stories lately. Meeting you has inspired me. Actually, I took one of your sketch pads and started a new book while you were sick."

"Huh." Wade finished feeding the fire, closed the stove's lid, and moved over to the table. He pulled out a chair, turned it backward, and straddled it. He ogled Faith's long, lovely legs and grinned at her, the grin of a satisfied male who has marked his territory.

"What are *you* grinning at?" Faith asked as she carefully laid slices of bacon in the warmed pan.

"I was just thinking about how much better your books will be now that you actually have some hands on experience," he said, waggling his eyebrows at her. "We'll have to continue your education and make sure we don't miss anything. I want to give you lots of background to pull from."

Just the thought of taking Faith to bed again was making him hard.

Faith stepped over to him and leaned down to kiss him. "I can't wait," she murmured.

"Neither can I." Wade jumped up from the chair and grabbed her arm. "Turn off the bacon. We have other business to take care of first."

An hour later they lay on their backs beside each other, panting and sweaty. Faith wondered if she could even walk after this last bout of sex play. Wade was a thorough and attentive lover, much to her delight.

Richard flitted into her thoughts and she wondered what he would have been like in bed. Somehow she thought he would be somewhat boring—dry and clinical and too focused on himself. She hoped her sister was happy with her choice. Hope may have done Faith a big favor by taking Richard off her hands.

Faith's body felt like limp rubber. She moaned

and rolled off the bed. "That's enough for me for a while. I need to clean up and eat. How about you?"

Wade groaned. "I'm not sure I can move. Give me a minute and I'll join you in the shower."

The following two weeks passed in a haze of hiking and sledding, love-making and writing. Faith had never felt so happy or contented. For the first time in her life, she felt good about herself. She felt as if she belonged someplace and with someone.

Wade carved while Faith wrote, each focused on and lost in their work. In the evenings they played games and talked about everything under the sun—except Susan. Wade refused to discuss his dead wife and eventually Faith stopped asking.

One night, after a particularly tender round of lovemaking, Faith lay with her back tucked against Wade's chest, his arm looped lightly over her hip. She snuggled closer and pulled Wade's calloused, scarred hand to her lips and kissed the pad of his thumb.

Wade?"

"Mmmm?" Wade was mostly asleep.

"What happens after ice out?"

"What do you mean?" Wade mumbled into his pillow.

"I mean . . . what happens with us? I-I've fallen

in love with you, you know. Do you . . . . feel anything for me?"

Faith held her breath. It had not been easy to reveal her feelings for the man beside her, but her love for Wade continued to grow stronger every day and she felt she couldn't ignore it any longer.

Nor could Faith ignore the fact that Wade had the power to hurt her in a way she had never before experienced. Richard's betrayal had hurt, but her heart had not been broken when she had discovered that he had married her sister.

She knew now that she had never loved Richard, and if she had gone through with the marriage they both would have been miserable.

She waited for Wade to answer her question.

Wade pulled his hand away and tucked it close to his body.

"I haven't really thought ahead that far," he said slowly. "I can't tell you that I love you, Faith. I'm not sure that I'm even capable of love. That's why Susan wanted a divorce. She claimed I didn't love her enough because I always put my job first, and now I think maybe she was right."

"I see." Faith tried to keep her voice matter of fact to hide the sudden stab of pain that pierced her chest like a spear of ice. You can't force someone to love you, she told herself.

But the thought did little to alleviate her pain.

"I'm sorry," Wade continued. "I enjoy your company and making love with you, but I don't see myself making a long term commitment to any woman after what happened with Susan. I'm just not that kind of guy. I tried it and failed miserably."

Faith blinked back the tears that threatened to fall. Somehow she had allowed herself to believe that the time they had shared in Wade's cabin was the beginning of a long term relationship—that he had grown to love her, would want to marry her and raise a family with her. Foolish dreams based on nothing.

The truth felt almost too painful to bear.

"Thanks for being honest with me, Wade."Faith turned her face into her pillow and let her silent tears flow.

"Faith." Wade touched her shoulder lightly. "You're a very special lady. I just . . . "

"Forget it," came the muffled reply. "I'm sorry I brought it up. Go to sleep, Wade."

A tangible wall sprang up between them after that conversation. They continued to talk and make love, but Faith couldn't shake the sorrow she felt and Wade had visibly closed off a part of himself. Their conversations and lovemaking lacked the spontaneity and open joyousness they had first shared.

Faith began to pray for ice out. She needed to

leave Wade's cabin before her heart was completely destroyed.

On the fourth day after their conversation, Rafe flew over and dropped another package. Wade retrieved it alone. Faith made an excuse about needing to press on with her book.

In truth, it was becoming increasingly difficult for her to pretend that all was fine between them. Her writing had come to a standstill. How could she write a happily ever after love story when the one she was living could only end in heartache?

Faith stood on the porch after Wade left, watching his tall, strong body snowshoe out to the package, pulling the toboggan instead of riding it down the hill.

She had given her heart to Wade without reservation. Whether he meant to or not, he had marked her as his, and she could never belong to another.

Before Wade, she had been alone because of Hope's underhanded manipulations. Now she would face the future alone because she could never love any man but Wade.

There was more. Faith had asked about Wade's love because despite the fact that Wade had always been careful to use a condom, she suspected she was carrying his child.

She placed her hands over her womb and gently pressed.

It was early days yet, but her intuition and the number of days that had passed since her last period told her she could be pregnant. If she was indeed pregnant, she would have Wade's baby, raise it alone and give it all her love.

The only question was whether or not to tell Wade he was going to be a father.

Out on the bog, Wade bungeed the package to the toboggan and headed back toward the cabin. Lately he had felt confused and frustrated and stupid, all emotions that made him act cross and short-tempered.

He liked Faith Donahue. He liked her a lot. He had never had so much fun with a woman, in or out of bed. Faith was intelligent and interesting and easy to be with.

He enjoyed being with her—more than he had any other woman if he was honest with himself.

Not that he had many to compare her with. He believed in monogamy. He and Susan started dating in high school and continued to date until they were married. Then she was brutally murdered and he lost any interest in women.

In addition to the fact that Susan's death was his fault, he just wasn't good husband material.

Hadn't Susan asked for a divorce a short time before she was killed?

Obviously he lacked some essential trait that made for a happy marriage.

He had loved Susan. He had thought he was a good husband right up until the evening she told him she wanted a divorce. And he had been determined to fight for their marriage. He had tried to talk her into giving it another try.

Susan had refused, said she wanted to be free to marry another. They had married too young, their marriage was a mistake, they didn't love each other enough, blah, blah.

And then she'd been murdered before they could work it out.

Wade gave his head a shake and clenched his jaw. No. He refused to put himself in that situation again, to open himself up to pain and suffering and guilt. He was better off living out his life alone, here in the cabin where he couldn't hurt anyone else.

Only he had hurt Faith. He knew that he had. She tried to act as if nothing had changed since the night she had told him that she loved him, but everything had changed.

The easy warmth of their friendship had disappeared from the relationship and he felt guilty again. Guilty because he had hurt Faith even though he had tried not to.

"Aw, hell." He wished the snow would melt so she would leave and he could enjoy his solitude again.

Wade carried the package into the cabin and unpacked it without Faith's help. He pulled food-stuffs and newspapers and magazines, candles and toilet paper from the box.

"Where would you like these?" he asked Faith, holding up a box of tampons.

"I'll take them." Faith stowed the toilet paper and tampons under the bathroom sink, then grabbed the newspapers and a cup of tea and sat by the wood stove to read.

It took a full week for the significance of the tampons to hit her.

"How did your cousin Rafe know to include tampons in the box of supplies?" Faith stood in front of Wade, seated on his carving stool, and waited for an answer.

Wade's hands stilled. He looked up at Faith and saw the confusion and fear that clouded her beautiful eyes. Aw hell. It was time to tell her. Maybe this was what she needed to show her that he wasn't worthy of her love.

"I called him," he answered casually, continuing to carve at the piece of basswood in his hand so he wouldn't have to see the look in her eyes when she learned the truth. He blew at the loose shavings.

"I figured you'd been here about a month and you would need them."

Faith's body went cold and rigid. She had to force herself to breath. "You called Raphael? How-how did you do that? You told me you didn't have a phone in the cabin."

Wade looked up then and made himself look Faith in the eye even though he knew what was coming. "I didn't lie. I don't have a phone in the cabin. I keep a cell phone up at the old fire tower on top of the mountain. That's the only spot high enough to get cell reception around here."

"So . . . I could have called Richard when I first got here. Why didn't you want me to call my fiancé?"

Wade shrugged. He couldn't say for sure why he hadn't wanted Faith to call her fiancé to come get her. There was something about her situation, about the way her sister had brought her out here and left her to die, that didn't sit right with him, and until he had figured it out he had wanted her here where he could keep an eye on her.

"I probably would have told you about the phone eventually, but I got sick if you remember, and then I liked having you around, and *then* you found out that your *fiancé* had married your sister. After that there didn't seem any point in telling you."

The disappointment in Faith's eyes made Wade

feel six inches tall and that made him want to lash out at her.

"What?" he asked. He glared at her. "I told you I was a worthless piece of shit, remember? You should thank me. I saved you from making a big mistake. Any man who would marry Hope when he could have you instead is either an idiot or a fool or both."

Wade flung the carving to the floor and stood up. "I'm going for a hike." He pulled on his outerwear and slammed the cabin door behind him.

13

———

Faith began to tremble after the door slammed behind Wade. A solid lump of pain grew in her chest until it nearly choked her.

Wade had lied to her. Not telling her he had a phone may have been a lie of omission, but in her mind it was a lie all the same.

The time had come for her to leave. She could no longer bear to be alone in this cabin with Wade and ice out was still a couple months away.

Why did she have to wait for ice out? A road led into the cabin and had to be connected to a main road. Wade's story that she needed to wait for ice out was a load of bull crap. Another of his half truths.

Faith moved around the cabin gathering the few things that were hers.

She stopped beside the sun-drenched bed with its beautiful blue and white quilt. Her heart ached in her chest. She picked up Wade's pillow with shaking hands and held it to her face, breathing his scent deep into her lungs so she would never forget how wonderful he smelled.

She replaced the pillow and gently smoothed its surface, then turned resolutely away from the bed. The bed where Wade had taught her about love and sharing one's body.

Faith pulled her wool pants, and then her wind pants, on over her long underwear. She would have to borrow Wade's shirt and a sweater and his parka. He'd be okay with his down vest and windbreaker until she could mail his things to his cousin Rafe.

She pulled on her boots and balaclava and stepped onto the porch. She needed to leave a note, or Wade would come looking for her. He may not love her, but he was the most responsible man she had ever known. He would worry unless he knew she was safe.

Faith walked back into the cabin and pulled a sheet of paper from the back of the sketch pad she had been using to write her latest book. She would take the manuscript too, she thought. No point in leaving it behind.

She dashed off a quick note. She didn't have much to say, she found. She told Wade that she would ship his clothes and extra snowshoes back to

Raphael when she got home and thanked him for everything he had done for her. After a moment's thought she simply signed it 'Faith.'

As an afterthought she added a PS. "Your carvings are worthy of an art gallery. I hope you show them one day."

Faith took a last look around the cabin that had become an unexpected and beloved home to her. "I wish you peace and happiness, Wade," she said aloud.

Her heart felt as if it would split in two. She hurried from the cabin before she could change her mind, put on the old snowshoes and followed the tree-lined, snowy drive to the unplowed minimum maintenance road.

Three hours later she reached a main, plowed road.

Wade returned to the empty cabin shortly after Faith had left. He read her note and started after her, then changed his mind. He headed up to the old fire tower instead and called his cousin.

The fire tower had been Wade and Raphael's favorite hideout. Located on the very top of Mulligan's Mountain, the wooden structure had been abandoned in the latter half of the 1900s. The cousins had found it in their early teens and claimed it as their own.

It was still Wade's favorite spot for thinking. Although the wooden tower had begun to rot and was no longer safe to climb, the mountaintop afforded a panoramic view of the surrounding valleys and mountain peaks.

He had come here often after Rafe had rescued him from near death.

After Susan's funeral, Wade had tried to hide from the memory of her last words in a whiskey bottle. He made it eighteen months before the other members of the force refused to partner with him because he had lost all self control and could no longer be depended upon.

Wade didn't care. He had wanted to die, wanted to escape the accusation that haunted him day and night, and he continually placed himself in dangerous situations.

One night he pushed his luck too far and was shot in the shoulder for his effort. His superiors took advantage of the injury to force him to retire.

Wade had crawled farther into the bottle then and waited to die. But for some death did not come easy.

Rafe had tracked him down, dragged Wade from the hovel he had called home and brought him to the family cabin to dry out. Gradually the cabin's solitude brought Wade a small measure of peace.

He had renewed his interest in whittling to help pass the long hours and take his mind off the desire for a drink. His grandfather had first introduced whittling to Wade when he was nine years old and deemed responsible enough to have his own knife.

His grandfather always had some small wooden trinket he was working on in his pocket. He'd take it out whenever he was idle, said it helped him think. For Wade it had the opposite effect—it gave him something to concentrate on other than his thoughts and memories.

"Aw, hell."

Wade stood with his arms loose at his sides and gazed out over the snow-covered peaks that extended into the distance until they faded into the dusky blue horizon.

Why did Faith have to land on his doorstep? He had been getting along just fine on his own. He *needed* the peacefulness of solitude. He enjoyed being alone. He enjoyed not feeling responsible for anyone but himself.

Being with Faith had made him forget about his failure with Susan and that was wrong. He could never forget. Because of him, Susan was dead. Before Faith showed up Susan's ghost had lived on his shoulder, always with him.

In the last few weeks there had been entire days when he hadn't even thought of his dead wife.

He told himself that he had done the right thing. He couldn't promise love to a fine woman like Faith when he had failed so miserably in the past.

She was far better off without him. He was damaged goods, and she was too special to chain herself to him.

He only wished the ache in his chest would go away.

Faith popped out of the wood's road onto the main, plowed road with relief. The three hour hike had not been particularly difficult other than she had to fight the urge to turn back every step of the way.

A black SUV sat parked on the side of the main road. As Faith bent to remove her snowshoes, a tall man with dark blonde hair emerged from the driver's side.

"Are you Faith Donahue?" he asked.

Faith stepped out of the shoes and straightened to inspect the man.

"Who are you? How do you know my name?" She didn't like being out here in the middle of nowhere with a strange man.

She looked up and down the road. It was wide and white with packed snow as far as she could see in both directions. Tall banks of plowed snow backed by a thick wall of evergreens lined the sides.

There were no cars coming and there was nowhere to run. The man could easily grab her and no one would know what had happened to her.

The man stopped moving forward and held up his hands, palms facing her.

"Don't be alarmed, Miss Donahue. Wade called Rafe to meet you and give you a ride home, but my cousin had a charter and couldn't get away so I came instead. My name is Mayhew. I grew up with Rafe and Wade. I'm the third cousin. We used to call ourselves The Three Mountaineers." He smiled, showing perfect white teeth.

Mayhew reached into his coat pocket and pulled out a cell phone. He held it toward her.

"Here. You can call Rafe, or anyone else if you'd like to let them know where you are. I'm not planning to abduct you, or hurt you. Honest."

Faith stared at the stranger, trying to take his measure. It was not something she was very good at, she admitted to herself ruefully.

Take Richard, the only man she had thought she knew and understood. He had turned out to be someone else entirely.

Other than height, there was little similarity

between Wade and Mayhew. Where Wade's face consisted of hard planes, Mayhew's was softer. He was handsome in a pretty boy kind of way, without that underlying masculinity that Faith found so exciting in Wade.

The man's words finally penetrated her thoughts. Wade had called to arrange a ride for her. She felt warmed that Wade had shown concern for her and at the same time it made her feel unaccountably sad. Rather than coming after her he had hiked back up the mountain to call his cousin.

If she needed more proof that Wade felt fine with letting her go, surely that was enough. The knowledge jabbed her heart with icy precision.

She stared silently at Wade's cousin for several long moments.

Mayhew broke the silence first. He gestured toward the vehicle. "I'll take you to Rafe's. His wife Sarah is home with the kids. Maybe after you meet her you'll feel more comfortable about letting me drive you home."

Faith nodded. "All right." It could be hours before another car came along, and even then it might not stop to give her a ride.

Her only choice was to accept Mayhew's offer of a lift or walk the forty miles to Greenville where she could rent a car. She knew that Hope must have taken her car back to Portland.

Had she sold it, figuring Faith would never

need it again? Or had Hope kept the car because it was a newer model than her own?

It wasn't important at the moment. She'd deal with everything when she got back to her house in Falmouth.

They drove the hour to Greenville mostly in silence. Mayhew made a few attempts to draw Faith into a conversation, but she kept her answers to his questions short and one syllable. After a while he gave up.

Eventually Mayhew pulled the SUV into the driveway of a neat, two-story frame house on the western edge of town and parked. To their right lay the large, unbroken expanse of snow-covered Moosehead Lake.

Faith blinked against the sun's blinding reflection off the lake. She could feel the north wind, unchecked by trees as it roared down the length of the lake, push against the SUV.

"This is Rafe and Sarah's place. You'll like them."

A small, blonde woman came to the front door and stepped onto the small deck that fronted the house. She waved at the SUV and called to Faith to please come inside, then turned and went back into the house.

Faith thanked Mayhew for the ride and climbed out of the vehicle. She hesitated, uncertain. She felt shy all of a sudden. How much had Wade told

Rafe and his wife about her? Did they know she and Wade were lovers?

Had been lovers, she corrected herself.

She wished she had her own car and could simply make her excuses and leave. She realized then that she didn't have a credit card or cash to pay for gas, not even her driver's license.

Hope had taken everything when she had abandoned Faith in the woods.

Now Faith saw that without identification, her body—if it were ever found—would have been labeled a Jane Doe. Chalk one more black mark on her sister's side of the board, Faith thought bitterly.

She had no choice but to take whatever help these people offered.

Faith walked slowly up the steps and rapped softly on Sarah's door. It opened immediately and a small, dark-haired girl with large brown eyes stared at her.

Faith smiled down at the girl. "Hello. My name is Faith. May I come in?"

The girl gave a solemn nod and ran down the hall, leaving the door open behind her.

Faith stepped into the entryway, still smiling. She could see a piece of a sunny kitchen at the end of the hall, a living room through a door to her right, and a playroom scattered with toys to her left. A staircase straight ahead led to the second floor.

"Come back to the kitchen!" called the woman from the rear of the house. "I'm feeding the baby and he gets cranky when I stop."

Faith removed her boots and made her way down the hall. She glanced at the living room as she passed the door. A large screen television dominated one wall but this was a family that also read. Books and magazines were piled on various small tables. Plump pillows sat in every chair and the couch. The room was warm and welcoming, a place to relax.

She continued down the hall into the kitchen. The bright and cheerful room echoed the warm and welcoming feeling of the living room and some of Faith's tension left her body.

The Winehursts' kitchen ran the entire width of the rear of the house, with an eating and cooking area on one end and a fireplace with sofa opposite. Large glass doors along the back wall led to a fenced, snow-covered yard. Three snowmen of various sizes faced the house.

The little girl who had opened the door for Faith sat on the floor studiously coloring and humming to herself. A box of crayons sat half-empty beside her as she selected and rejected them.

The blonde woman sat at a round oak table with a high chair containing a chubby blonde toddler pulled close to her side. She was spooning orange goop into the toddler's mouth. The toddler had orange hands and cheeks and a streak of orange in his short curls.

It was a happy family scene.

A fierce longing filled Faith. This is what she wanted for herself. A real family. A loving, safe home. She put her hand over her abdomen and made a silent promise to the child she carried that she would give him or her the same secure love that filled the home of Wade's cousin.

The woman looked up at Faith and smiled. "I'm Rafe's wife, Sarah. This is Ethan, and Erin let you in. The water in the tea kettle is hot." She pointed to a counter. "Cups are hanging there and tea bags are in that cupboard. Help yourself."

The toddler grabbed the spoon and tried to pull it to his mouth. "Are you hungry, Ethan? You'd think we never fed you." The toddler slapped the tray with his open palm and opened his mouth.

Faith smiled at Ethan's antics. She found the tea bags and made herself a cup of mint tea, then joined Sarah at the table.

"I'm Faith Donahue. Your children are beautiful," she said.

Sarah beamed at her. "Aren't they, though? I know I should be more humble since I'm their mother, but Rafe and I make pretty babies. I'm fortunate that Ethan here will eat everything. He loves carrots."

She laughed as Ethan grabbed for the spoon again. Sarah fed it to him and gave Faith a speculative look.

"So tell me, how did you end up at Wade's cabin? You could have knocked me over with a feather when Rafe told me his cousin had a woman living with him. Wade has been . . . well, let's just say that he's had a rough time of it. He's been alone too long and we were beginning to wonder if he would ever recover from what happened to Susan."

Faith told Sarah that she had gotten lost in the woods and Wade had rescued her from freezing to death. As nice as Sarah seemed, she hadn't planned to go into the sordid details about her sister Hope and *why* she had been lost in the woods.

But Sarah turned out to be a good listener and Faith found herself telling her about Hope abandoning her and then about Wade's fever.

Sarah didn't interrupt with questions while Faith talked. She merely nodded or shook her head in sympathy.

"Wow," she said when Faith finally wound down. "It sounds as if you were both lucky. You would have died without Wade's help, and he would have died without yours."

Sarah placed her hand briefly over Faith's. "Thank you for staying with him and nursing him.

We love Wade. Rafe and I are both close to him. He's godfather to both our children, although he hasn't even met Ethan yet and he's barely seen Erin. He took Susan's death hard. He was almost dead himself when Rafe went down to Boston and dragged him back here."

"Do you think . . . " Faith hesitated. "Do you think that he could really be responsible for Susan's death in some way?" Faith asked.

Sarah scooped some carrots off Ethan's chin and fed it to him while she thought about her answer.

"It's possible that someone Wade put away, or someone who had a relative put away, killed Susan for revenge. Wade looked into all that and couldn't come up with anyone. Nor could the detectives assigned to find her killer. But Rafe and I believe it's the most likely scenario. Whoever killed her had a lot of rage."

"Did Wade tell you that Susan blamed him for her murder?" Faith asked.

Sarah nodded and cooed encouragement to Ethan as she fed him another spoonful.

"Yes. He told us what she said." Sarah hesitated. "It's not right to speak ill of the dead, but Susan . . . well, let's just say that Wade and Susan probably shouldn't have married. They were young, and Susan was looking for a way out of here.

"She wanted to live in the big city, and Wade

was leaving for Boston to follow his dream of being in law enforcement. Their relationship would have fizzled out naturally from being separated, but Susan followed him to Boston."

Sarah gave Faith a considering look. "Wade would hate to hear me say this, but he's the kind of guy who takes care of people. He married Susan because she needed him to take care of her."

Faith thought about the way Wade had saved her and held her on his lap when she was upset, and the way he had made love to her. She had to agree with Sarah, the man was a nurturer, even if he didn't know it.

"Were they in love?" she asked.

Sarah hesitated. "I couldn't say, I didn't see them together much once they left Greenville. They had a typical high school romance, and of course this town is so small there isn't a large pool to choose from. We all hung out together and were good friends. I'm sure Wade told himself he loved her and gave the marriage his best effort, but his career took up a lot of his time and energy.

"Personally I think after Susan got a taste of city life she wanted more and Wade wouldn't give it to her. He's a country boy at heart. He didn't care for the social scene—he preferred to stay in when he wasn't working or come back here when he had a few days off. Susan told Wade she wanted a divorce. A week later she was dead."

Sarah changed the subject and the women talked easily while Ethan finished his lunch.

Sarah's obvious pleasure at being a wife, mother, and homemaker drew Faith to Sarah. Under different circumstances she felt they could have been friends.

Without being aware of it, she rubbed her abdomen, thinking of Wade's baby, barely the size of a peanut but already very real to her.

"Are you all right?" Sarah's big blue eyes were filled with concern and sympathy. "Do you have a stomach ache? I have some ginger ale if you want. My mother always gave it to me and my siblings when we had an upset stomach."

Faith shook her head. "Thank you, but I'm fine. Just tired. I really should get headed home. Would it be possible for me to borrow a car and gas money? I lost everything when I was in the woods and I don't have any way to rent a car."

"I'll drive you."

Faith hadn't heard Mayhew come in. He stood in the kitchen doorway, leaning against the jamb. How long had he been there listening?

She felt uncomfortable at the idea of spending three hours in the car with a strange man but she couldn't see any alternative. She couldn't call Richard to come get her, and she wouldn't call Hope, even if her only other option was to hitchhike home.

Thank you," she said after a moment's hesitation. "I'd appreciate that."

Mayhew turned and left the kitchen. Faith stood and pushed her chair beneath the table. She stroked one of Ethan's soft cheeks with the back of her fingers.

"Good-bye, little man. Be sure and eat all your vegetables for your mother and grow up to be big and strong like your Uncle Wade, okay?"

Faith smiled at Sarah. "Thank you for the tea. I enjoyed talking with you."

Sarah placed a hand on Faith's arm. "I don't know what happened at the cabin with Wade, Faith, but I can tell you that Rafe says he's never heard Wade sound happier than he has in the last few weeks. You're good for him. I wish you'd think about that and consider coming back."

Tears threatened to clog Faith's throat. She had the overwhelming urge to confide everything to this woman, but she stopped herself. She didn't want Wade to know about the baby yet. Maybe not ever. That was something she still needed to work out.

No matter what she decided about the baby, she wouldn't be back. She could never force herself upon a man who didn't love her.

She made herself smile. "Good-bye, Sarah." Faith turned away from the table and followed Mayhew back out to the SUV.

14

"So why'd you leave the cabin? Wade is a good guy." Mayhew popped the question after two hours of silence.

Faith continued to stare out the side window and shrugged one shoulder. She had no intention of sharing anything about her experience at the cabin with a virtual stranger.

"My cousin is a good man," Mayhew repeated.

Faith turned to look at him. Apparently he wasn't going to let it go.

"Wade is a good man" she agreed. "But it was time for me to leave. I have a book that's ready to publish. I need to get back to my life. And I don't think Wade wanted me there any longer. I had invaded his privacy long enough."

Mayhew's pale blue eyes hardened. "Are you

sure? What did Wade have to say about you leaving?"

Faith turned away and stared out her side window again. The highway was edged with long stretches of pine forest occasionally broken up by a farm or small town. The same thing she'd been staring at without seeing it since they'd left Greenville.

"What business is it of yours?" she asked, not looking at him. "Wade and I barely know one another. It was time for me to leave."

"Sorry. Rafe and Wade and me, we grew up together like brothers. My father was the younger brother of their mothers. That's why we all have different last names. Wade went through a terrible experience in Boston, you know. I feel protective toward him. He always looked out for me in school. I don't want to see him hurt again. He almost didn't survive his wife's betrayal."

"Betrayal? What do you mean?" Faith turned to look at Mayhew.

Mayhew's hands tightened on the steering wheel. "Wade gave his heart to Susan and she broke it. When she asked for a divorce she really hurt him. He's just beginning to get whole again. Are you breaking his heart by leaving?"

Faith gave a choked laugh. "Hardly. You don't have to worry about Wade, Mayhew. He was very clear about the fact that he doesn't want me. I imagine he's relieved to have me out of his life. Now if you don't mind, I'd rather not talk about Wade anymore. What do you do for work, Mayhew?"

To Faith's relief, Mayhew dropped the subject of Wade. They talked about inconsequential things until he pulled up in front of her little house. Faith fairly leaped out of the SUV, she was so glad to be home.

She pulled off Wade's sweater and parka, pulling the folded pages of her latest manuscript from the parka's inside pocket.

"What's that?" asked Mayhew.

"A new book I worked on while I stayed at the cabin. Don't worry, I didn't steal any of Wade's sketches."

Faith laid the sweater and parka on the passenger seat. "I had to borrow these. Please see that they're returned to your cousin. Thank you for the ride, Mayhew."

Faith turned away from the SUV and hurried up her walk. Someone had shoveled the snow, she noted, wondering if one of the neighbors had kept it cleared for her.

She reached behind the window shutter and grabbed the spare key she kept hung there in case she lost her keys and put the key in the lock.

Behind her, Mayhew's SUV roared away.

Faith breathed a sigh of relief. She was glad to be rid of Mayhew and his probing questions.

She unlocked the door and returned the key to its hiding spot before she forgot, then stepped inside.

A startled cry escaped Faith's lips. Her hand flew to her heart as she took in the chaos that greeted her. She stepped forward and tripped over the wood and iron coat tree that she had bought at a local auction.

She picked up the coat tree and set it back in its corner. The hall mirror and several framed prints of her book covers lay smashed on the floor. Her hall half-table and the pottery bowl that held her car and house keys and sunglasses lay in pieces.

Faith took a shaky breath and picked her way through the debris. A quick tour showed similar destruction throughout the downstairs of her cozy house. The house stank of rotten food and perfume.

Every dish in the kitchen lay broken on the tile floor. The curtains had been ripped from all of the windows and soaked in catsup and food. Napkins and placemats were slashed.

The couch and chair cushions in her sitting room were also slashed, the stuffing pulled out and thrown about. Every picture or decorative item Faith had lovingly collected had been destroyed.

She made her way up the stairs to the second

floor, her body trembling with shock. All of the clothing in her bedroom had been pulled from the closet and drawers and slashed to ribbons, then tossed onto the floor. Bath salts, oils, and perfume had been dumped on her prized oriental rug.

The mattress, bedding, down pillows and comforter had also been slashed. Fluffy bits of white down lay everywhere. It skittered away from her as she walked through the room.

Faith looked at the destruction, barely able to breath. The degree of hatred shown here took her breath away. This was not the work of an anonymous housebreaker. There was only one person who knew her well enough to hate her this much.

Her sister Hope had done this.

Hope must have used the emergency key, a key that Faith had foolishly entrusted to her, to enter the house after she had left Faith stranded in the woods. Hope had wantonly, and with great malice, destroyed Faith's home after leaving her for dead.

No, Faith corrected herself, Hope had destroyed everything but the bronze silk sheath that Faith had bought to get married in. That Hope had taken for herself, she thought bitterly.

"Oh no!" Faith whirled out of the bedroom and crossed the hallway to the second bedroom which she used as her office. Destruction reigned there as well.

Every book that filled the bookcases which

lined her office walls had been pulled off the shelves, torn apart, and tossed into a pile. Faith spied the cover of her most recently published book. Hope had taken a heavy black marker and crossed out Faith's name with hard, angry strokes.

She searched for her writing computer but couldn't find it in the mess. Everything else from her desk had been destroyed. A sense of panic began to build in Faith. She had put the finishing touches on a new novel the day before she and Hope had left for their camping trip, planning to upload it to the various book-selling sites when she returned.

Faith forced herself to slow down and sift through everything until she knew without a doubt that not only the computer but her external back-up was missing as well.

It was more than Faith could bear. She collapsed onto the floor and cried—great, wrenching, loud sobs that ripped at her chest and throat. Tears and mucus streamed unchecked down her face.

It was all too much.

Her sister had left Faith to die in the Maine woods.

Then she had married the man that Faith had been engaged to.

Faith had lost her heart to a man who didn't want her and had returned home only to find that her sister had destroyed Faith's sanctuary.

On top of it all, she was sure she was pregnant with Wade's baby.

Faith cried until her body felt like a wrung-out dishrag and she began to hiccup. The hiccups hurt. She dragged herself to the bathroom and drank from the faucet until they stopped, then splashed water on her face.

She winced when she looked up and saw herself in the cracked mirror. Her eyes looked bruised and bloodshot and glazed with shock, and the smattering of freckles on her nose stood out against her pale skin.

She picked up a shredded towel and wiped at her face, then blew her nose into it and tossed it back to the floor.

Closing the cracked toilet lid—Hope had certainly been thorough—she sat down to think.

Fortunately Falmouth was a small, self-contained suburb compared to its neighbor, the city of Portland. They knew her by sight at the town hall and the local bank branch. She could replace her identification and get new bank cards and some cash from her accounts.

A strange calmness came over Faith. She realized that she had lived her entire life on pins and needles, waiting to see what Hope would do to her next.

Now Hope had done her worst and Faith was still here. She had survived her ordeal in the Maine woods. She could clean up this mess and start anew.

She would write more books. And they would be better books because of the experience she had shared with Wade. Hope had done her an unintended favor.

The baby was also a gift, Faith realized. She would not be alone any longer. She would have a child to love and nurture and provide for. Together they would be a family, something that she had always yearned for.

Faith left the bathroom and pulled down the trap door that led to the small attic. She unfolded the hinged steps and climbed them, unsure what she would find. To her relief, Hope had missed the attic.

Faith hauled down a box of clothes that she had stored after losing some weight. They would be a little loose on her slimmed-down frame, but they would tide her over until she could either order more online or shop for a wardrobe to replace the one Hope had destroyed.

She tossed everything from the bathroom into the hallway, keeping a broken bar of soap and a couple shredded towels to dry off with, and took a long, hot shower.

Afterward, feeling clean and less shaky, Faith found a scrap of paper and a broken pencil in the office. She sat on the floor to make a list of the things that needed to be replaced immediately.

A knock on her front door interrupted her before she could finish the list. Faith froze. What if it was Hope? Had her sister somehow discovered that Faith had survived and returned to her home? A cold fear coursed through her body.

Then she realized that Hope had no further reason to return to Faith's house, there was nothing left for her here. And if she did, Hope had a key to let herself in. She wouldn't bother to knock.

Faith stood and looked out the front window but the roof over the entryway prevented her from seeing who stood at the door. She ran down the stairs. Looking out the small sidelight, she saw the elderly woman who lived next door.

Faith had made friends with the reclusive Mrs. Reynolds, often inviting her to share a cup of tea when she took a break from writing.

Mrs. Reynolds enjoyed talking over plot issues with Faith and Faith had found her neighbor to be an intelligent and pleasant woman.

Faith opened the door wide. "Mrs. Reynolds! I'm so happy to see you."

Mrs. Reynolds craned her skinny neck to peer behind Faith. Her pale eyes opened wide, then narrowed to angry slits. She tapped the end of her cane hard on Faith's step.

"I had a feeling I shoulda called the police when I saw that no good sister of yours show up when you weren't home."

"You saw Hope?" It surprised Faith to realize that she still held a tiny kernel of hope that a stranger had destroyed her home, even while she knew beyond any doubt that it was her sister.

Mrs. Reynolds pursed her lips and nodded. "I came over and asked about you. I was worried, you see. Your sister told me to mind my own business and slammed the door in my face. Piece of work, that one. An ice cube wouldn't melt in her mouth. Hard to believe you share the same DNA."

She reached out a hand and patted Faith's arm. "Come over to my place, dearie, and we'll have a cuppa and figure out what to do about that mess."

Faith blinked back the fresh tears that sprang to her eyes. Her emotions felt so raw. "Thank you, Mrs. Reynolds. I'd like that."

She closed the door behind her. "I guess there's no point in locking up—there's nothing left worth stealing."

She followed her neighbor down the short walkway and up the next one. Mrs. Reynolds's house was a duplicate of Faith's: three rooms downstairs with two bedrooms and a bath on the upper floor. But where Faith had kept her decor bright and uncluttered, Mrs. Reynolds went for heavy damask drapery and solid, dark furniture.

Knickknacks covered every horizontal surface in her neighbor's house. Mrs. Reynolds was especially fond of owls and had been collecting their images for decades in every form possible. Hundreds of the nocturnal creatures stared at Faith as she followed the old woman through the house.

They eventually settled with their tea in the room Mrs. Reynolds referred to as her parlor.

"So . . . when did Hope come by the house?" Faith asked.

"Let me see. It's been a while. You've been gone longer than I expected. You told me that you and that sister of yours were going winter camping near Greenville for the weekend and you'd be back late Sunday night. I must have seen Hope here on that Monday."

So, Faith thought with a spurt of anger, Hope didn't waste any time destroying my home. She must have felt certain that I would die up there. Her hand shook slightly as she lifted the tea cup.

"You said you spoke with her?" she asked aloud.

"Oh yes, of course I did," replied Mrs. Reynolds. Faith knew that the elderly woman kept watch on the neighborhood out her parlor window. She had her favorite chair pulled close to the glass so she wouldn't miss anything.

"I asked your sister where you were and she said that you had taken off somewhere to do research for your next book. When I asked her where you went and when you'd return she told me to mind my own business, then she slammed your door in my face. That was the last I saw of her."

Mrs. Reynolds gave Faith a shrewd look. "Course I knew you hadn't done any such thing. You always let me know when you're going to be away so I can keep an eye on your place. But she *is* your sister, so I didn't listen to my intuition. More fool me. I'm so sorry, dear. I coulda had her caught red-handed tearing your place apart."

Faith gave a weak smile. "That's all right, Mrs. Reynolds. How were you to know?"

An intense sadness washed over Faith. "I never realized just how much Hope hated me," she said softly.

Mrs. Reynolds handed Faith a plate of store-bought vanilla sandwich creme cookies. "Eat. You look peaked. That's what my mother used to call it when one of us girls seemed wiped out."

Faith took a cookie and managed a wan smile. "I need to replace my driver's license and bank cards and get some money and call somebody to haul everything away. And a locksmith. I need to replace the locks immediately. I don't want Hope to be able to get inside my house again unless I invite her. Could I please borrow your car for a few hours?"

"Of course you can, dear. You know I don't have any use for it." Mrs. Reynolds had had her license taken away from her three years earlier when she turned ninety, but she had refused to give up her old Cadillac, claiming the car was part of her family.

The car was a classic, with large tail fins and big leather bench seats, and finding room to park the monster was always tough, but Faith needed a car and she had driven the Caddy many times. Mrs. Reynolds liked her Sunday drives, and often coerced Faith into driving her in the Caddy through the countryside or up the coast.

Faith finished the tea while Mrs. Reynolds caught her up on the neighborhood gossip. She promised her neighbor that she would come over as soon as she had things settled again and grabbed the keys and left.

<h1 style="text-align:center">15</h1>

<hr>

IT TOOK the remainder of the day for Faith to get new bank cards, identification, and a new cell phone. Faith slept in Mrs. Reynold's spare room, grateful she didn't have to sleep in the midst of the destruction in her home.

She called a handyman for hire company and arranged to have the owner meet her at her house right after lunch the following day.

At the appointed time, a middle-aged, capable looking man with a round face and twinkling pale blue eyes showed up at her door. Faith liked him immediately.

When the handyman walked inside the house, his eyes widened with shock and he asked her if the police had finished with the crime scene.

Faith looked at him in surprise. The thought of filing a complaint against Hope for the vandalism she had wrought hadn't even crossed her mind. She turned the idea over in her mind, then decided against it.

Hope would have an alibi and a good story that would make Faith look the fool. She didn't need to hand her sister another victory.

She shook her head ruefully. "No, I didn't bother to call the police. I know who did this. Trust me, there's nothing I can do about it. I just need you to haul everything away so I can get on with my life."

The handyman looked skeptical, but they agreed on a price and he left, promising to return the next day with a dump truck and two extra men.

Not wanting to impose on her neighbor's hospitality two nights in a row, Faith walked two miles to a small family-run motel on Route One and booked a room for three nights. She had an early dinner at a nearby diner, took a hot shower, and fell into bed.

She woke the next morning to sunshine streaming through the thin window curtains.

Faith lay in bed and thought over her situation. Today she would borrow the Caddy again and purchase furniture in Portland to replace what Hope had destroyed, as well as dishes and kitchenware.

She had decided not to replace everything at once. She would buy only what she needed to be comfortable. If she decided not to stay in her house she wanted to make moving as simple as possible.

The thought of selling her home didn't feel as difficult to contemplate as Faith would have expected. She had been so proud when her book sales grew to the point where she could purchase the small house. Decorating and choosing furnishings that reflected her personality had been fun and satisfying.

This morning she found it hard to care about the house. She could chalk that up to Hope, she thought. Her sister had invaded and destroyed any sense of peace that Faith had ever enjoyed in her first real home.

She let the thoughts of Hope go. She didn't feel ready to face that can of worms yet. She would have to confront her sister eventually, but she planned to build up to it.

Did she really want to sell her house and move? She thought of her neighbors, mostly elderly, and other than Mrs. Reynolds, most of whom she knew only well enough to wave hello to. She wouldn't be leaving any close friends behind. She didn't have any close friends.

She could write and publish her books any-where, as long as she had a fast internet connection. She could even move to Greenville, rent a small house, and see how she liked living there.

If she moved to Greenville then she'd be able to share the child with Wade.

Maybe she and Sarah could become friends and the baby would grow up with cousins.

Faith laughed at herself as she climbed out of the bed. Fat chance of that fantasy coming true, she thought. Why would anyone from Wade's family want anything to do with her once they learned Wade himself didn't?

Faith firmly pushed thoughts of Wade away. She had plenty of time to figure out what to do about letting Wade know about the baby. She had more pressing matters to deal with first.

Faith dressed, ate a big breakfast at the diner, and walked back to Mrs. Reynold's to borrow the Caddy. By late afternoon she had purchased a new bed and dresser, sofa and matching recliner, kitchen table with four chairs, and all the odds and ends that people need every day and never think about until they aren't there to use: towels, forks and spoons, glasses, tea mugs, soap, hairbrush, comb—the list seemed to go on and on.

The furniture stores promised to deliver her purchases the following day. Faith drove the loaded Caddy back to her house and parked out front. The dump truck had already left with the remnants of her life filling its bed.

She walked into the now empty house and stood in the entryway, suddenly unwilling to move further inside.

The house stood silent around her; not even the refrigerator hummed. Hope had unplugged it and allowed the contents to spoil. The handyman had promised to remove the rotted food, but the odor still hung in the empty house.

Faith sighed. She'd better scrub the refrigerator first.

The urge to erase Hope's presence from the house grew until it overwhelmed Faith. With the house completely empty this was the perfect time to scrub away all traces of her sister.

Even if she ended up selling, she would have to thoroughly clean the house, she reasoned. Galvanized into action, Faith carried the cleaning supplies, new vacuum cleaner, mop, rags, and broom that she had bought earlier into the house and set to work.

The locksmith showed up and changed the front and rear door locks. At Faith's request he installed extra deadbolts on both doors and left her with two sets of keys. Knowing that Hope couldn't enter her house unless Faith let her in eased some of her tension.

Five hours later she called for a delivered pizza and ate it sitting on the butcher block counter she had installed when she first bought the house. She felt tired but still had more to do.

By one a.m. she had finished scrubbing the house from top to bottom. The smell of rotten food had been replaced with the fresh scent of orange oil cleaner. Her arms and shoulders ached with exhaustion, but she felt pleased and satisfied.

She had taken the first step to begin building a new life and she felt better than she had since leaving Wade's cabin.

Faith carried the remainder of her purchases in from the Caddy and returned the car to its garage. She kept the keys. She had an errand to run later that day and Mrs. Reynolds had encouraged her to use the car for as long as she needed.

She made a mental note to keep an eye out for a new owl to add to her neighbor's collection as a thank you gift.

Staggering with weariness, she made a bed on the floor from the new blankets and pillows she had purchased and lay down. Sleeping on the floor reminded her of sleeping next to the wood stove at Wade's.

A longing so intense she could barely draw a breath filled her chest and tears pricked her eyelids.

She wondered how he was doing. Pretty well, she imagined. His unwanted house guest was gone and he could return to his solitary ways. She wondered what he was carving. He had only roughed out his next project right before she left and she hadn't asked him about it. Now she wished she had.

She pictured his hard, roughened hands with the small white scars and remembered how they had felt on her skin when he made love to her body.

She ached to feel his touch again, his heavy weight bearing her down into the mattress, making her feel safe. Making her feel desirable and loved.

Only she wasn't loved, was she? That was a dream, nothing more than a plot line for one of her romance novels.

"Oh, Wade," she whispered into the darkness, and silently cried herself to sleep.

Wade sat in the reading chair next to the wood stove, his long legs stretched out in front of him, and stared into the fire. God how he wanted a drink! He hadn't been able to relax since Faith had left the week before.

What was she doing, he wondered? He had called Rafe to find out about Faith's house, not that he had told his cousin that was the reason for the call. Wade had claimed that he was making sure Faith had made it home safely.

He hadn't been happy to hear that Mayhew, not Rafe, had driven Faith home.

It wasn't that he didn't trust his cousin, but Mayhew was a handsome man, always with a new woman in his life. A player. Wade had asked Rafe to take Faith home because Rafe was happily married and deeply in love with his wife. Wade knew he wouldn't make a pass at Faith.

Mayhew had nothing to prevent him from making a play for an attractive woman, and God knew, Faith was a very attractive woman.

Rafe had only been able to tell Wade that Mayhew had delivered Faith to her doorstep, forcing Wade to call Mayhew and try to get more details. But Mayhew had been curt on the phone, telling Wade that Faith Donahue was no good for him and he needed to forget her.

Well, he already knew that didn't he? Unfortunately, forgetting Faith wasn't that simple. Her presence filled the cabin even without her there.

He saw her sitting in the other reading chair, curled up like a cat before the fire. He saw her in his bed, cooking at his side, seated at the kitchen table, wrapped in a towel after her shower. He pictured her with her head thrown back and screaming with glee as they tobogganed down the hill in front of the cabin.

Mostly he saw her beneath him in bed while he moved inside her, her blue-green eyes dark and glazed with desire and tenderness.

Faith had made him laugh, had made him feel like a carefree teenage boy again. And she was smart. She challenged him and showed a real interest in a variety of topics.

She had made him feel like a god in bed, worshipping him with those sultry, tilted eyes and her eagerness to learn and please. He missed her trust in him and her complete abandonment to the pleasure they gave each other.

Wade looked down at the half done carving in his hand. He missed Faith. He hated to admit it, but there it was. She had shown up in his life and changed him.

Before her arrival he had been going through the motions of living. Faith had reengaged his relationship with life. She had made him care again.

He turned the carving over and rubbed his thumb over its surface. It was a female torso, from shoulder to upper thigh. Faith's torso—a body he knew intimately, having explored every glorious square inch with his hands and mouth.

He eyed the carving critically. There needed to be more definition where her rounded bottom met the back of her thigh—a spot he especially liked to stroke and nuzzle.

"Aw, hell."

She was better off without him. She had said she loved him, but her memories of their time together would fade. She'd meet someone else eventually and forget him.

Wade wished he could say the same for himself. Something told him that he had been given a special, beautiful gift and he had let it fly away.

16

THREE MONTHS HAD PASSED since Faith's return to Falmouth, three busy months as she pulled the pieces of her life back together and worked on her new book.

Just like in academia, where the rule "publish or perish" governed a professor's success, in the world of romance fiction an author needed to keep publishing books regularly or the fans forgot them and went elsewhere to appease their need for entertainment.

Faith's latest manuscript was essentially the story of her and Wade Elliot, only in her make believe version the tale would end as all romances should: with a happily ever after.

She still missed Wade. Small memories of him

intruded on her all through the day and night. It seemed that everything reminded her of him.

Taking a shower, she remembered the feel of his hands sliding down her back as he soaped her body. Making breakfast, she was reminded of how carefully Wade made bacon and egg sandwiches, working at the stove dressed in his faded jeans and nothing else, the muscles in his broad shoulders moving smoothly under his skin.

Picturing Wade's shoulders reminded her of the puckered scar from the bullet he had taken.

She could manage the memories a little easier during the daytime as she could keep herself busy with work and putting her life back together. Night time was a very different story.

She missed Wade's warm, strong body and making love with him. She missed being held by him while she slept. She missed . . . everything about him.

Faith sighed, pushed away thoughts of Wade, and entered the office building in front of her.

The history department was housed in one of the state university's oldest brick buildings. Although several rounds of modernization had taken place over the decades, the building retained its original 1800s character.

Faith admired the wide, reddish-brown wood trim with its carved egg-and-dart design and the ornate balustrade under her hand as she climbed the wide staircase.

She had been there twice before, both times to meet Richard before a dinner date. His office occupied the southeast corner of the second floor.

Three other offices opened off the central, wood-floored, second floor hallway. A tall window at the near end of the hall cast a pale, murky light that washed out the weak light from the nearest wrought-iron wall sconces. The hall smelled of floor wax and dusty books.

Faith stopped outside Richard's door. She had eventually come to realize that she needed to face him in order to firmly close this chapter of her life.

She needed to hear the truth from Richard's own lips. She needed to hear why he had married her sister so soon after Faith's disappearance. Most of all she wanted to know why he hadn't looked for her.

She also needed to return the engagement ring. She pulled the ring from her jacket pocket and examined it. The simple gold setting held a sapphire instead of a diamond. It was all that Richard said he could afford.

Faith hadn't minded. She had worn the ring proudly, only taking it off to do the dishes. Afraid that she might lose it in the snow, she'd also removed it before her trip north with Hope.

She had been surprised to find the ring underneath the refrigerator when she had scrubbed the house.

Two co-eds walked down the hall giggling together, books held against their chests, and disappeared down the stairs.

Faith stared at Richard's name on the frosted glass that filled the upper half of the old oak door. DR. RICHARD TRASK: MEDIEVAL STUDIES, had been stenciled in a bold black arc. Parts of TRASK had flaked off.

Richard must hate that, Faith thought. He had been so proud to get his name on the door.

A white haired professor came out of the office opposite and hurried to the elevator at the end, her high heels doing a rapid rat-a-tat that echoed in the nearly empty hall.

The elevator, a moderately recent installation required to bring the building up to disability standards, had eliminated two offices and caused a great deal of snarky back-biting over who best deserved the remaining spaces.

Richard had smugly gloated when he secured the corner office, Faith recalled, a quality that she had found unattractive at the time.

There was no point in putting the confrontation off any longer. She raised her hand and knocked sharply.

"Come in," called a male voice. The voice lacked the depth and raw masculinity that had marked Wade's voice. It sounded weak and querulous to her ears. Why hadn't she ever noticed that before?

Faith pushed open the door and stepped inside, closing the door behind her.

"Yes? What is it? I don't have all day. I'm a very busy man." Richard sat at his desk with several old books open before him. He had yet to look up at his visitor.

Faith took the opportunity to inspect the man before her. His bent head showed a small, shiny bald spot in the mouse brown hair. His hands looked small, white and soft. His narrow shoulders sloped. He would soon become a stooped hunchback if he didn't fix his posture, she observed dispassionately.

Weak. Everything about Professor Trask looked washed out and weak. Why had she never noticed *that* before?

The answer was obvious—because she'd nothing to compare him to and now she did.

Richard lifted his head. "I said, what do you wa —Faith? Is that you?" The surprise in his small brown eyes hardened to contempt. "What are you doing here?"

"I came to return this." Faith stepped forward and set the ring on the corner of Richard's desk. "I also wanted to ask why you never came to look for me, and why you married Hope. I thought you loved me."

"Look for you?" The scorn in Richard's voice was palpable. "Why would I waste my time looking for a woman who had run from me rather than keep her promise to marry me?"

Faith furrowed her eyebrows. "I didn't run. Hope left me to die in the north woods."

Richard made a sound in his throat. "Don't lie. Hope told me the truth. She told me how you only agreed to marry me because you wanted the prestige of marrying a man with his doctorate degree. She also told me you changed your mind and left town rather than face me. At least you had enough compassion not to leave me standing at the altar. I should probably thank you for that."

Faith's mouth dropped open. She clamped it shut immediately. She looked at Richard, her gaze steady. "We weren't getting married in a church, Richard. How could I leave you at the altar?"

Richard waved a hand in the air. "Semantics."

Faith looked steadily into her ex-fiancé's eyes. "Let me be sure I understand you. Hope told you a story about me and you believed her without waiting to hear my side of it?"

"Why would your sister lie about something like that? Of course I believed her. I consider myself fortunate that she agreed to marry me in your place to save me from any embarrassment."

Faith pursed her lips, then nodded slowly. "I

see. I guess Wade was right. Hope did me a favor by marrying you. You don't deserve me. I hope you and my sister are very happy together, Richard. I wish you the best."

She saw something flicker in Richard's eyes and smiled. "Ah. I see you are already learning about Hope's true nature. Well, good luck to you. I have a feeling you're going to get exactly what you deserve."

Richard scowled up at Faith. "You have a lot of nerve coming to my office to harass me. If you don't leave I shall summon security."

"No need. I've said and heard all I need. Goodbye, Richard."

Faith sailed out of Richard's office with a wide smile on her face and a light heart.

Later that night Faith received a puzzling email from one of her fans.

Have U seen this?

The email contained a link to Amazon. Curious, Faith clicked on the link. It showed a book titled *Favorite Night*. A romance written by author Hope Donovan.

Faith's hand shook as she clicked the "look inside" link and read a few familiar pages. The book was a word for word rip off of one of her own romance novels titled *Favorite Knight*.

She stared at the page for several minutes, unwilling to believe that on top of everything else her sister had plagiarized one of her books.

She clicked on the author bio with a shaking finger. Her sister Hope's face smiled out at her.

"Oh no." Faith blinked back tears of anger. How could Hope do this to her? Surely even her sister would draw the line at plagiarism.

She quickly typed Hope Donovan into Amazon's search bar and hit the search button. Seconds later all the works published under Hope's pen name filled the screen.

There was only one that wasn't a plagiarized version of Faith's books. The book that Faith had been about to publish after her camping trip with Hope.

Hope had stolen that book outright and put her own name on it.

Faith felt icy cold with anger. She closed down the computer and sat staring out the window at the rooftop of the house opposite.

What did authors do when their work was stolen?

She needed to contact Amazon and the other booksellers she used and alert them to the situation. She also needed to hire an intellectual property lawyer and tell him the whole sordid story and see if there was any legal way to stop her sister.

Once she knew her legal rights, she would confront Hope.

17

PATCHES of bare ground were beginning to show in the open spots of the woods surrounding Wade's cabin. The ice on the bog had softened and become too punky to risk walking on.

Wade had a love/hate relationship with this time of year. With the snow melt came all the fresh scents of bare earth and the promise of new life, something he loved.

The snow was wet and harder to navigate with snowshoes, but there wasn't yet open water so he could use the kayak. Getting around was problematic, but he hated being stuck inside.

The days warmed while the nights were still cool. Flocks of ducks and geese traveled north as new food sources became available, their honks and chortling calls filling the air. The male cardinals were a brilliant red and singing, hoping to attract mates for the upcoming nesting season.

Wade didn't want to think about mates.

The empty space that Faith had left inside his chest had not filled in since she had left.

He pushed himself harder physically than he ever had, trying to tire himself out so that he could sleep without missing her warm body next to his.

He cut and chopped enough firewood for the next two heating seasons, cleaned out the storage space under the deck, hiked up to the fire tower daily—sometimes more than once.

He had taken to sleeping in his reading chair so he wouldn't have to face his lonely bed, but nothing helped ease the ache and sense of loss.

He talked to Rafe and Sarah more often, and had even stooped so low as to ask Sarah what she and Faith had talked about. It didn't surprise him that Sarah had liked Faith and thought that Wade should pursue her, but Sarah didn't know that Wade had betrayed Faith's trust.

The truth filled him with shame. He had behaved no better than Faith's sister and fiancé.

He knew he was in serious trouble when he willingly embarrassed himself by asking Rafe to include some of Faith's books in a care package. Rafe, bless his heart, had said nothing, and the next package had contained six of Faith's romances.

Romance. Jesus. He, Wade Elliot, tough guy, ex-detective, was reading romance. What kind of man was he anyway? Only sissy-pants men read romance.

Sissy-pants and him, he amended. To make matters worse, he actually enjoyed Faith's writing. He had expected emotionally gushy bodice rippers, but Faith's books were more mystery or suspense, with a romantic core running through well thought out and intelligent plots.

He flipped open the back flap of the book he was currently reading and stared at Faith's head-shot. He tilted turquoise eyes stared back at him.

He liked Faith Donahue. He liked her a lot. She was the whole package. Beautiful, smart, open and honest, sincere, fun, loving.

So why wasn't she still here with him? For the billionth time, Wade recalled the painful conversation where she had declared her love for him and he had told her he could never love her.

Then she had found out about the phone. That he had kept its existence a secret from her. He had essentially lied to her, and why? Why hadn't he told her about the phone and allowed her to call her fiancé?

Because even then he had wanted her to stay. He hadn't realized how lonely he'd been until she came into his life.

What a fool he he had been. Faith was the best

thing that had ever happened to him and he'd blown it.

He made a disgusted sound in his throat and looked around the cabin for yet another project to distract his thoughts away from Faith.

The bathroom could use a thorough scrub down, he decided. He hadn't cleaned the cabinet under the sink since last spring.

Wade gathered the cleaning supplies and headed to the bath.

He removed the towels and rugs and hung them on the porch rail to air in the sun, then knelt before the cabinet and hauled out the items stored there. Toilet paper, toilet brush, extra shaving cream and razor blades, tampons, plungers, the new box of condoms he'd never opened because he and Faith had not had sex after she learned that he had lied about the phone.

He scrubbed the empty cabinet and began to replace the items. His hand hovered over the un-opened box of tampons. Should he keep them in case Sarah got caught unprepared while visiting?

Wade frowned at the box, then shoved it back into the cabinet. Waste not, want not. He was a good New Englander. His Puritan ancestry ensured that he had been brought up not to waste anything with a potential use.

He finished the task and returned to the

kitchen where he put the cleaning supplies back under the sink. Now what?

Wade stood staring out the front window at the bog. Small pockets of open water were appearing in the snow-covered ice. A pair of blue-wing teal settled gracefully onto one, their brilliant spring colors flashing in the sun.

Something was niggling at the back of Wade's mind. He had learned to pay attention to that sensation of something important lying just out of reach. It had helped him solve a difficult case on more than one occasion.

He cleared his mind and let his thoughts drift. It had something to do with being wasteful. He turned and let his eyes drift over the cabin without resting upon anything.

Something in the bathroom had caught his attention.

The unopened box of tampons, that was it. Why did they bother him? What about them? Tampons weren't something a man had to think about, let alone worry about. They were firmly in the woman's domain, a fact of being female that he was grateful he didn't have to deal with.

His eyes continued to drift until they landed on the calendar hanging on the wall next to the refrigerator. He walked over to it, pulled it off its small nail, and carried it back to the table.

Leaning on one hand he flipped the pages back

to the day he had found Faith nearly dead from hypothermia. Then he flipped forward to the day she had walked out.

Seven weeks. Seven weeks and the box of tampons had never been opened. Of course that could simply mean that Faith had an irregular period, or the hypothermia had thrown off her regular cycle.

The unused tampons could also mean that she was pregnant.

Wade had been careful to use a condom without fail, but the original box of condoms had been sitting under the bathroom sink for at least three years. And who knew how long they'd sat on a store shelf before Rafe had bought them.

The thought had never occurred to him that they might have passed their use by date.

A dizzying shock zipped through Wade's body. Faith could be carrying his child.

He stood abruptly, staring at the calendar but not seeing it. Instead, he saw Faith's long legs and slim body, naked beneath him. Her beautiful turquoise eyes looking up at him, glazed with pleasure.

Oh man, he was so stupid.

He couldn't blame Faith for this. The woman had been a twenty-eight year old virgin for crying out loud. She had no reason to use birth control and every reason to believe that Wade had dealt with the risk of pregnancy by using condoms.

Faith pregnant. Wade could hardly breathe. "Aw, hell."

He forced himself to take several deep breaths. He had to find out if Faith Donahue was carrying his child. He had to know. He had wanted children with Susan but she had not wanted any. After her murder he had felt grateful that there were no children for him to deal with.

Susan had been right to refuse him a family, Wade realized now. He was rarely home when he had worked as a detective. The brunt of childcare would have fallen on her shoulders. At that time he would have made a lousy father.

But not now. Now he would welcome the opportunity to share in the raising of children. He could watch their child while Faith wrote. He could find a non-demanding job and work nights and be a Mr. Mom during the day.

The thought made the tension in his chest loosen. He would do right by Faith. Wade took several long strides to the door and pulled on his outerwear.

He had to get up to the fire tower and call Rafe to meet him. He needed a ride. It was time to pay Faith a visit and find out if she was carrying his child.

If she was pregnant he would ask her to marry him and he wouldn't take no for an answer. She loved him. She had told him so. She would marry him.

The thought cheered Wade tremendously. He whistled as he climbed Mulligan's Mountain and placed his call.

The next morning Wade locked the cabin and headed to the highway. He checked off a list in his head: wood fire out, perishables in compost pile, water pipes shut off and drained, gear stowed away under the porch, windows and door locked.

He carried four changes of clothes in his backpack, his carving knife, small chisels, and the torso he was working on. He also had a gift for Faith. She had admired the lynx and he wanted her to have it. He would give it to her as an engagement present.

Wade made excellent time getting to the rendezvous point but Rafe wasn't there. He paced up and down the road, anxious to get to Faith. Two cars stopped to offer him rides. He thanked them and sent them on their way.

Finally Rafe showed up. Wade was surprised to see Sarah and the baby with him.

"What are you doing here?" he asked as he tossed his pack into the rear of Rafe's SUV. He climbed into the passenger seat and reached back to tweak the baby's chubby knee. "Hi big guy, it's nice to finally meet you."

Ethan kicked his feet and gurgled a reply and gave Wade a wide, drooly smile. Wade smiled back.

He wouldn't mind having a son. A girl would be nice, too. One with tilted blue-green eyes and a wide, lovely smile.

"Well?" he asked Sarah. "Were you feeling housebound? Where's Erin?"

"Erin is with a playmate. I knew that unless I came along and heard the story first hand I'd never get my questions answered," Sarah replied. "So, why are you leaving the cabin? Not that I'm not ecstatic that you're finally rejoining the world, but I know you, Wade Elliot. There has to be a compelling reason."

Wade turned back to the front. "There is." He hesitated. Did he really want to confess to Rafe and Sarah that Faith could be pregnant with his child because he had trusted old condoms?

The need to share overcame Wade's need to hide his shortcomings.

"I think Faith might have been pregnant when she left," he said. "If she is I intend to make her marry me."

Sarah gasped. Rafe gave Wade a quick, surprised look before returning his attention to the road. "Marry? Am I hearing right? You've been alone in the cabin for over three years now, cuz. Do you think you might be overreacting? And what makes you think she'll agree to marry you?"

Wade shrugged. "I don't see why not. She told me that she loved me and a child needs a father."

Neither Winehurst spoke for a moment.

"Do you love her, Wade?" Sarah asked after a few minutes of silence.

"I don't believe in love anymore, Sarah. I like Faith very much. That's enough. I loved Susan and you saw how that worked out. She wanted a divorce and now she's dead because of me."

Behind him, Wade heard Sarah make a disgusted sound in her throat. "You and Susan never should have married," she said. "Susan only married you to get out of Greenville. I don't believe she ever intended to go the distance with you, to have a family. You should have given her the divorce when she asked."

"That may be," Wade said quietly. "But I couldn't admit defeat until Susan and I gave our marriage every chance."

He glanced back at her. "I didn't realize you felt that way about Susan, Sarah. It's not important why Susan married me. My point is, I learned my lesson from that experience. I don't intend to repeat that mistake."

"We all felt that way about Susan," Rafe told him. "She used you, Wade. She was always a user. I'm surprised a smart guy like you couldn't see it."

Wade said nothing. He looked out the side window, hoping his cousin and cousin-in-law would drop the subject.

Maybe he should have taken one of the other

rides that had stopped and offered so he wouldn't have to explain himself to his family.

Why did Sarah care if he loved Faith? A child needed a father. That was the important thing. He was trying to step up to the plate and do the right thing by the woman he had impregnated.

If Faith was pregnant. He didn't know the answer to that yet.

"What if she's not pregnant, Wade? Will you still ask her to marry you?" Sarah asked, as if reading his thoughts.

Wade loved Sarah, but sometimes she was too sharp for his liking. She had a way of looking inside him and asking uncomfortable questions. She would make a good detective, he thought ruefully.

"I don't know, Sarah. I haven't thought that far ahead. First I need to find out if Faith is carrying my baby."

"How can you be sure it's yours? Wasn't she engaged to be married when you saved her life?" Rafe asked.

"I'm sure. Drop it okay? What's Mayhew up to this week?"

To Wade's relief the grilling stopped and they discussed other subjects. They had known one another all their lives and they slipped easily into a comfortable camaraderie. Rafe and Sarah were more than family, they were also his closest friends.

Despite that, Wade only half-listened as they talked.

Rafe's charter flight business had grown to the point that he was considering hiring another pilot.

Sarah told him about Ethan and Erin's antics and caught him up on old schoolmates' whereabouts.

As the miles passed beneath the SUV's tires the tension began to build in Wade's chest again.

What if Faith was pregnant and refused to marry him? What would he do then? It surprised him how badly he wanted a child.

He simply wouldn't take no for an answer. Somehow he'd make her see that having two parents were more important to a child than love.

18

———

FAITH WAS UPSTAIRS WRITING when she heard the knock on her front door. She lifted her head and frowned. She wasn't expecting visitors and decided to ignore whoever it was. She hated to be interrupted while she was working. Her neighbor Mrs. Reynold's knew not to stop by until after dinner when Faith had wrapped up her work for the day.

She turned her attention back to her computer screen and tried to pick up the thread of the scene she was working on.

An honest to god pirate. Who would have . . . the knock came again. Louder, more insistent. More of a pounding, than a knock. A demand that she answer.

She knew that it wasn't Hope or Richard. Hope would never pound on a door in such an unladylike fashion, and Richard didn't have the strength. He would never risk those soft hands of his.

What if something terrible had happened to Mrs. Reynolds? Faith sighed, hit SAVE, and closed the laptop.

She ran lightly down the stairs, grumbling at the unknown intruder.

Her usually flat belly was just beginning to swell and round. Fortunately the fat clothes she kept stored in the attic still fit around her waist. She had made one shopping trip for maternity clothes and hadn't been able to make herself buy anything. The knit pants with the expandable front panel had been just so . . . ghastly.

She had decided to switch to loose dresses when her belly grew too large to zipper her pants. She'd be roundest over the summer and early fall, so dresses would also be cooler as well as comfortable.

Faith had made her first appointment with an obstetrician, a gray haired woman who had not batted an eye when Faith told her she planned to be a single mother.

Dr. Foley declared her fit and healthy and predicted no problems with the pregnancy.

The baby's first ultrasound picture stood in a wooden frame beside Faith's laptop. It looked like little more than a white blob in her womb, but the ultrasound brought home the reality that she was indeed carrying Wade's child.

She talked to the baby at night, rubbing her belly with smooth, slow circles, telling him (she didn't know the sex yet but felt sure she would have a boy) about her day and the plans for the following day.

She also played classical music while she wrote because she had read that it helped the fetus's brain develop. Whether that was true or just hokum she wasn't taking any chances. She would do anything to give her child a head start in life.

Her greatest fear was genetics. What if the genes that had created her twisted sister showed up in her baby? She didn't think she could survive loving another person who hated and tormented her in return.

Another bang sounded on the door as she reached it.

"I'm coming! Stop that racket, you'll wake the ba—" Faith pulled open the door and stared into Wade's deep blue eyes.

For a brief moment all the air was sucked off the planet.

God he looked good. He was taller and his shoulders were even broader than she remembered, the planes of his face sharper. His dark hair needed a cut and looked tousled, as if he had been running his fingers through it.

She resisted a strong urge to reach up and run her own fingers through his silky hair.

"Aren't you going to ask me in?"

Faith took a deep breath and tried to corral her emotions. What was he doing here? She hated the way she wanted to throw herself at him. Hated the way her pulse kicked up at the sight of him.

Instead of inviting him in she narrowed her eyes at him.

"Why are you here?"

Wade seemed unperturbed by her less than warm welcome. He reached out with both hands, gently grabbed her shoulders, and moved her aside.

"You look good, Faith," he said as he walked into her house and looked around.

She looked better than good, he had to admit. She looked amazing. He put his hands in his jeans pockets to keep from pulling her toward him and kissing her.

Faith closed the door behind him and he breathed a sigh of relief. She didn't hate him. She wouldn't let him stay if she hated him. That was a start at least.

"You look good too, Wade. Why are you here?" Her heart beat wildly against her ribcage and she thought she was going to be ill. Wade Elliot was the last person she had expected to find at her door.

Faith had hoped that her attraction to him had

faded with time and distance but it felt stronger than ever. She knew that Wade was dangerous to her heart and she needed to keep her distance from him or he would break it all over again.

They were still standing in the hallway.

"How about a cup of tea, Faith? I drove straight here from Rafe and Sarah's and I could use one. Is the kitchen back here?"

Wade didn't wait for Faith's reply. He knew that she might ask him to leave at any moment and he couldn't let that happen. Not until he had the chance to say his piece.

He headed down the hallway, checking the rooms as he passed. They seemed strangely empty and devoid of decoration, holding the bare minimum of furniture. If he didn't know that Faith had lived here for several years he'd guess that she had only recently moved in.

It was a cute little house other than being mostly empty. He liked the oak floors and the varnished wood trim. The windows were clean and everything looked well cared for.

Faith reluctantly followed Wade into the kitchen and put on the tea water. She pulled two mugs from the cupboard and added teabags, then pulled out a chair at the table and sat, saying nothing all the while. She had asked Wade a question and she wanted an answer.

Why was he here? His presence messed with

her head and her heart and she didn't like it one little bit.

"Somehow the place doesn't look like I imagined," Wade said as he joined her at the table. "I expected your house to reflect more of your personality. I thought it would be brighter and more cheerful. This is almost . . . austere."

"Yeah, well, Hope left me an unexpected surprise. Not that she thought I'd ever return. She destroyed everything in the house. Why are you here?"

Wade's eyes darkened with anger. "What did your sister do?"

Faith gave up. Obviously Wade would not answer her question until he felt ready. She stood and turned off the boiling tea kettle and poured hot water into the mugs, waited a minute, and then carried them to the table.

"When Mayhew dropped me off I had to use the spare key I kept hidden outside to get in, because as you know Hope took everything of mine with her when she abandoned me."

Faith couldn't look at Wade's face. She glanced out the kitchen window and watched the swollen buds of the lilac bush rock in the breeze.

"Apparently leaving me to die wasn't enough. She came back here and destroyed everything I owned except for the dress I bought to be married in. She took that and my computer with her. I had to hire a handyman and two helpers with a dump truck to haul the pieces of my life away."

Faith's mouth twisted into a wry expression. Her sister's actions still hurt.

"Hope even broke my toilet seat. To add insult to injury, she plagiarized my books and published them under her own name *and* she stole my latest manuscript, the one I planned to publish when I returned from my trip north. She published that as well."

"Oh sweetheart, I'm so sorry." Wade's large hand covered one of Faith's.

She snatched it away and narrowed her eyes at Wade.

"Why are you here?"

Wade stretched his long legs out in front of him and crossed them at the ankles. He sipped on his tea and looked at Faith over the rim of his mug. Despite Faith's less than delighted welcome, he felt so damned happy to see her.

Faith tried not to notice how good Wade looked. The way he filled her kitchen. She could smell him—his soap and shampoo and that intangible masculine odor that made her tummy do flip flops.

She wanted to bury her face in his chest and feel his arms around her and she hated the feeling of vulnerability she felt around him.

Wade set down his mug and took her hand

again. She tried to pull away but he held tight. When she set her tea mug on the table he grabbed her other hand as well.

If it was possible, the blue of his eyes deepened. "Are you pregnant, Faith?" he asked.

The shock of the question nearly made Faith fall off her chair. She would have jumped to her feet if Wade hadn't been holding her hands. She blinked several times and her mouth dropped open.

"How . . . how did you know?"

Satisfaction crossed Wade's face. He had guessed right. He looked into Faith's beautiful wide eyes and rubbed his thumbs over the soft skin on the insides of her wrists. God he had missed her!

"I found the unopened box of tampons in the bathroom. It took me a while to understand what that meant, but I finally realized that there was a reason you hadn't opened them. I didn't do a very good job of protecting you. I'm ashamed of that. I was the experienced one, I knew those condoms were might be too old but I . . . well, let's just say that I was irresponsible and leave it there."

Faith stared at Wade. He had figured out she was pregnant because of the tampons? And he was taking responsibility?

She wasn't sure what to think or feel. She still couldn't wrap her mind around the fact that Wade was sitting in her kitchen.

Wade cleared his throat and gently squeezed Faith's hands.

"I want to do the right thing by you and the baby, Faith. Our child needs a father and things will be easier for you if you have a husband to help you raise it."

"Raise *him*," Faith corrected. "The baby is not an it. I don't know the sex yet of course, but I've been talking to him. I think I'm going to have a boy."

"Okay. Him. Things will be easier for you if you have a husband to help raise *him*. I want you to marry me, Faith."

For a moment—oh such a brief moment!—Faith's heart soared. Wade wanted to marry her. There was nothing she wanted more.

Then her sense of reason penetrated her high. The man she loved with all her heart hadn't said anything about loving her. Faith's heart plummeted.

"Why?" she asked aloud. "Why do you want to marry me?"

Wade's black brows furrowed. He scowled at her. What didn't she understand? He thought he had clearly laid the situation out for her.

"What do you mean, why do I want to marry you? I just told you why."

"You want to marry me so the baby will have a

father and to make things easier on me." Her voice sounded flat to her ears.

Wade must have caught her tone because he let go of her hands.

"Yes. I want to be a part of my son's life."

Faith nodded slowly. Her gaze never left Wade's eyes.

"Do you love me?" She watched his eyes cloud and shutter. His lips thinned into a straight line.

"You know I'm not capable of that, Faith. I can promise to always be there for you and the baby. I'll never cheat on you with another woman, and I promise to be a good father."

Faith stood and set her mug in the sink. She kept her back to Wade.

"It's not enough. Thank you for the offer, Wade. It's very responsible of you, but I need more. I need to be loved. I deserve to be loved."

She squeezed her eyes shut to stop the tears that threatened, then opened them and turned around.

"I will certainly let you be a part of our son's life. I'll sell this house and move to Greenville to make it easier for you to spend time with him. I can write and publish anywhere, so I think that my moving makes more sense than you relocating down here."

Wade sat at the table and stared at Faith. He felt

cold. Cold and numb with shock. He had been so sure that Faith would accept his marriage proposal. He had spent the drive down to Falmouth making plans to renovate the cabin and put on an addition so they would have plenty of room for the baby.

He couldn't believe she had rejected his offer. What sort of fool behaved that way? Anger washed through him and he stood abruptly.

"I see. Well, I guess I'll be going." He grabbed a pencil and pad of notepaper from the table and wrote, tore off the paper and set it on the table.

"That's my cell number. Call me when you're ready to move and I'll give you a hand." He pulled the paper back and wrote two more numbers.

"These are Rafe's and Sarah's numbers. They can give you some idea of what's available for rentals in town."

Wade stared at Faith's eyes, wide and shiny with tears. He didn't understand. Why did she have to be so irrational? He could only give what he had to give.

He turned on his heels and walked down the hall to the front door, leaving Faith in the kitchen.

He bent down to his duffle, removed something from the interior and set it on the small half-round hall table. Taking a deep breath, he walked out Faith's front door and managed to drive away without looking back.

He felt as if he'd been kicked in the gut.

Faith waited until she heard her front door close, then slowly walked into the hall. She leaned her forehead against the front door.

"Oh Wade." Had she made a mistake refusing his proposal of marriage? Couldn't it be enough if she loved him? Surely a marriage could survive if only one person loved.

But she knew that one person loving would never be enough for her. She desperately needed to be loved in return. She deserved to be loved in return.

Faith turned to return to the kitchen. Her gaze fell to the hall table. Wade's carved lynx, her favorite of his animal carvings, looked up at her.

She picked it up and held it to her heart. The tears fell freely and she could no longer hold back her sobs.

Once again her heart felt broken in two.

19

For the three days following Wade's unexpected visit, Faith threw herself into her work, determined to hold her yearning for and thoughts of Wade at bay. She was only partially successful.

Despite her efforts to get enough rest for her body to deal with the child growing in her womb, she lay awake at night, second guessing her refusal of Wade's offer to marry her and be a father to their baby.

During the days she wrote at a fever pitch, finishing one book, sending it off to her beta reader, and plunging immediately into another.

She filed a complaint with all of the websites that carried Hope's plagiarized versions of her novels. Both her and Hope's copies of her books were taken down until the matter could be resolved. It wasn't an ideal solution, but at least Hope wasn't making any sales on Faith's work.

Unfortunately, neither was Faith, but because she lived a frugal lifestyle and banked a large portion of the profit from her books, she had enough savings to live comfortably for at least several years.

There was nothing Faith could do about her latest finished work—the book sitting in her stolen computer that she had intended to publish after her trip north with Hope.

She had no means to prove that she was the true author of the book, and seeing it up for sale on Amazon with Hope's name on it twisted Faith's stomach into tight knots.

The intellectual property lawyer she had spoken with had been discouraging. Without her computer or the external back-up drive, she had no way to prove that Hope had stolen her work. All her notes were in the computer with the finished novel.

The lawyer recommended that she learn from the experience, and in the future back up her work to several locations, including one off-site in case she was ever robbed again.

Gradually the idea of moving away from Falmouth (and Hope) and creating a new life in Greenville, became more attractive to Faith. She contacted a real estate agent and made plans to list her little house.

The agent, a petite woman raised in Dallas, Texas, had obviously dyed blonde hair piled high and wore impossibly tall stiletto heels. She possessed an aggressive self-assurance that appealed to Faith, perhaps because at the moment Faith felt as if she was questioning everything about herself.

The agent told Faith that her house would sell quickly as it was located in a desirable location and neighborhood.

Faith agreed to have a couple small items fixed over the following week before they ran the listing.

Three days after Faith talked with the real estate agent, Hope showed up at her door.

Faith was upstairs writing when she heard a car park in front of the house. She peered out the office window, half hoping and half afraid that Wade had returned.

She watched Hope step out of the car and walk up the short walk while she thought about whether to let her sister in or ignore her.

Faith had put off her confrontation with Hope despite knowing it needed to be done before she moved. The problem was, she hadn't yet worked out exactly what she wanted to say to her sister.

She was afraid of Hope and she felt a great deal of anger toward her.

Anger over being left to die.

Anger over the plagiarized books.

Anger over the theft of her unpublished manuscript.

Anger over the destruction of everything she owned.

Anger over Hope's lies to Richard.

She did *not* feel angry over Hope's marriage to Richard. In fact, she should probably thank her sister for marrying Richard in her place. Since meeting Wade, Faith now realized what a namby-pamby Richard was.

She saw now that she never would have been happy with him.

In a twisted sort of way, Faith also owed Hope because Hope had left Faith to die. Because of Hope's hatred for her she had met Wade, experienced amazing sex, and was now carrying a baby.

She really should thank her sister for all that as well.

Besides the strange mix of anger and gratitude, Faith felt heartsick over the wasted potential of the sisters' relationship.

In her mind, sisters should be close, loving friends. The kind of friends who are there for each other when needed no matter what, simply because they were sisters. The kind of friends who shared their deepest feelings and secrets. The kind of friends who could be trusted no matter what.

Instead, Hope had made herself Faith's greatest

enemy. The harsh reality of Hope's deep hatred toward Faith made Faith feel weak and shaky.

Hope reached the front door and Faith heard her insert her emergency key in the lock. A small smile touched Faith's lips. Hope would not be happy when she discovered Faith had changed the locks. Hope did not like to be thwarted.

Faith ran down the stairs quietly and waited behind the front door. She still didn't know if she wanted to face her sister.

She heard Hope rattle the key and swear. Hope tried the key once more, then Faith saw her pass by the front window and look behind the shutter for the spare key that Faith used to hide there.

Hope pressed the doorbell. "Faith! I know you're in there! Let me in!"

Faith unconsciously placed her palm against her rounding belly and rubbed it gently.

"Faith! Dammit, let me in!"

"It's time for you to meet your aunt Hope, Simon," Faith whispered to the baby. She had been trying out boy's names for the last week and had recently settled on Simon.

Simon Elliot. She thought it had a nice sound; a name fit for a spy or a scientist or a great athlete. A strong name fit for a capable man.

"Don't be afraid, Simon," she continued. "I won't let her hurt you. After today you won't ever have to see her again, I promise." Faith unlocked the newly installed deadbolt and pulled the door open. She leaned on the door jamb and crossed her arms beneath her breasts, blocking Hope's way.

"What do you want?"

Hope was dressed as impeccably as ever in fitted taupe slacks topped with a pale rose sweater set. Her wavy blonde hair and carefully applied make-up, the look that reminded most people of an angel, failed to disguise the cruel glint in her wide blue eyes.

She eyed Faith's old sweatpants and man's chambray shirt with disgust.

"I see you still have no sense of fashion. I thought I did you a favor by destroying your wardrobe and giving you a chance to buy some decent clothes. You look like you shop in a rag bin."

Once upon a time Hope's words would have wounded Faith. Today she barely heard them. The fear she had always felt around Hope vanished.

"Only you would try to twist wanton destruction of my things into doing me a favor. You left me to die, Hope. You destroyed my house for the sheer pleasure of it. Why are you here?"

Faith felt so pleased to discover that she no longer craved Hope's acceptance and love that she almost smiled at her sister. For the first time in her life she honestly wanted nothing more from Hope than to be left in peace.

Hope must have sensed the change in Faith. A

small hint of uncertainty showed in her eyes, then disappeared. She tossed her head and lifted her chin, making her hair bounce over her shoulders.

Faith recognized the gesture as one Hope made when she was about to grind someone under her heel. She waited with almost clinical detachment to see what Hope would attack her with next.

"There you go, putting your unique spin on things again, Faith. Honestly, I think Mama must have dropped you on your head when you were a baby and scrambled your brains. You always were a little . . . slow."

"If I was dropped on my head I'm sure you did it," Faith said. "Again, why are you here? You've taken everything from me. What's left?"

Hope ignored her question.

"Aren't you going to ask me in, sis? It's very un-civilized of you to keep your only sibling standing on the door stoop. What will the neighbors think?"

Faith shrugged. "I don't really care what they think. What do you want, Hope?"

Hope's eyes narrowed with anger.

"You went to see Richard," she said.

"Yes. I wanted to return the engagement ring. It seemed wrong to keep it. So?"

"I refuse to talk out here. Invite me in."

Faith stared at her sister for several long moments, then shrugged and stepped back. She opened the door wider to allow Hope to enter, then closed the door and led the way into the living room, sitting on the edge of the new recliner and leaving the sofa for Hope.

She wanted to keep as much physical distance from her sister as possible.

As a child Hope had often hit and pinched the younger Faith. She hadn't touched Faith since they became adults, but the destruction of her things told Faith that Hope still carried a lot of unhealthy aggression towards her.

Faith absently rubbed the bump in her nose, a bump she had acquired when Hope had hit her in the face with a bat when Faith was seven and Hope eight. Of course Hope had twisted the story so their mother blamed Faith.

Her sister caught the movement and smiled.

"This is more like it. How about a cup of tea?" Hope asked.

"No, thank you. State your business and leave. You are no longer welcome in my home and I have things to do."

"Tut-tut. So rude of you, Faith. It seems my weakling of a sister has finally grown some backbone. All right, I'm here because I want you to leave my husband Richard alone. He married me, not you, and you have no business bothering him."

"I'll be happy to leave Richard alone. I have no interest in him. Is that all?" Faith stood, but Hope remained seated.

"How did you find out about the books?" Hope asked. "You really shouldn't have made such a stink about them. Now neither of us are getting any sales income from them. That was really quite stupid of you."

Faith looked down at her sister. Hope had always been jealous of Faith's successful career as a fiction writer. Hope had tried her hand at writing romance but had been unable to sell her books. Faith suspected that her sister's inability to love lay at the root of her lack of success.

"I have loyal fans, Hope," Faith answered. "Something you could never understand. I should probably tell you that I've hired an intellectual property attorney to deal with your theft of my books. Did you think that I would do nothing and allow you to steal from me?"

Hope shrugged one delicate shoulder and looked around the room at the bare walls and floors, the sparse furniture. Another small smile touched her lips.

"The house looks pretty bare, Faith." She stared at her sister, curiosity in her eyes. "How did you survive the north woods? I thought my plan was foolproof. You couldn't possibly have hiked out of there."

Faith stared at her sister, appalled by Hope's lack of shame over what she had done. How could anyone not see what sort of person Hope really was?

She suppressed a shudder. Hope felt no remorse, saw nothing wrong with trying to kill Faith.

Hope had no conscience, she realized. Her sister was a sociopath. Suddenly Faith wanted her out of the house. She stood and walked into the hall without answering Hope's question.

"Thank you for stopping by to check on me, Hope, but I have to get back to work." Faith opened the front door and waited.

After a minute Hope sauntered into the hallway and stopped beside the half-round table. Faith tensed as she picked up the carved lynx.

"Where did you buy this? It's quite well done." Hope flipped it over to look at the base.

"Who is WE?"

One of Hope's old tricks had been to pick up something of Faith's and then "accidentally" drop it so that it broke. Faith knew it had always been done on purpose by the way Hope smiled at the time.

Hope had that same look of anticipation on her face now.

Faith tried not to let Hope see how much she cared about the carving. If Hope thought she liked the lynx she would take great delight in destroying it.

She shrugged. "It was a gift from a neighbor. I

have no idea who carved it. The visit is over, Hope. Don't bother coming back, I won't let you in again. I'm through trying to have a real relationship with you. I'm taking out a restraining order against you and I'll call the police if you come back. You tried to kill me, you destroyed my home, and you married the man I was supposed to marry. I should thank you for that last one, by the way."

"Are you all right, dearie?" Mrs. Reynolds stood in the open doorway glaring at Hope. The fierce look in her eyes almost made Faith giggle, but the truth was, she wanted to hug her old neighbor for coming over to check on her.

"Hope was just leaving, Mrs. Reynolds. Weren't you, Hope?" Faith stepped closer to Hope, took the lynx from her hands, then stepped back to the open door.

Hope looked as if she wanted to argue, then changed her mind. She swept past Faith.

"You just leave my husband alone," she warned on her way out.

"Gladly." Faith stood beside her elderly neighbor and watched Hope drive away. When Hope's car turned a corner and they could no longer see it she put her free arm around Mrs. Reynolds and hugged her.

"Thank you, Mrs. Reynolds," Faith said. "Your timing couldn't have been more perfect."

Mrs. Reynolds looked surprised and pleased by

the hug. She patted Faith's arm with her multi-ringed hand.

"I'm glad I could help, Faith. That sister of yours is a real piece of work. I only wish I had called the police the last time she was here. How about a cup of tea?"

Faith smiled down at her neighbor.

"I'd love one. Come on in and I'll put the water on. I bought some chocolate biscotti at the bakery yesterday. I know you like them."

Faith listened to Mrs. Reynolds chatter with one ear while she went over Hope's visit in her head. She expected to feel some sadness, but instead she mostly felt relief that she no longer cared about her psycho sister. She had sincerely meant it when she told Hope not to come back.

Faith didn't care if she never saw her sister again. For most of her twenty-eight years she had struggled unsuccessfully to make Hope love her. Finally, she understood that Hope was incapable of caring for anyone besides Hope.

It was time for Faith to move on and build a new life in Greenville. While it was true that Wade didn't love her now, that didn't mean that he couldn't grow to love her in the future.

They would see each other frequently after the baby was born.

Who knew what the future held? If Wade asked her to marry him again she would probably say yes. She would rather live with the man she loved, even though he didn't love her, than live without him.

He had promised to be faithful. It would be enough. She wanted Simon to grow up with both his parents.

Faith felt buoyed by her decision about Wade and her new understanding of Hope. She felt elated about dropping her sister from her life and excited by the future. She had loyal fans and new books to write.

She'd have a child and Wade to love and nurture. She would give them both all the love that she herself had been denied.

She felt relaxed and happy for the first time in her life.

20

"Uncle Wade, I wanna ride my new bike." Erin tugged on Wade's pants.

Wade reached down and carefully lifted his grand-niece into his arms. He had been reluctant to handle Erin or Ethan at first. Erin felt so small and delicate, her slender arms and legs incredibly fragile, but Sarah had assured him that the children were tougher than they looked.

Erin patted his cheeks with both hands and gave him a smile that melted his heart. He had missed most of her first four years while he had fought the twin demons of guilt and grief.

He regretted that now, and was doing his best to make up for it. Since coming to stay with his cousin and Sarah he and Erin had become fast friends.

"Pleeze." Erin's brown eyes stared into his own.

Wade marveled at the way the youngster had already learned to wrap her daddy and uncle around her small fingers. He gave her a big smile and her eyes lit up with excitement.

"I'd love to watch you, honey," Wade said. "Would you like to ride your tricycle on the sidewalk? Does Mommy let you?"

Wade was babysitting for Erin while Sarah took Ethan in for a routine doctor's check up. He had hightailed it back to the cabin after Faith's refusal to marry him, but unlike previous times he had not found solace in the cabin's isolation so he had returned to Greenville while he figured out what to do next with his life.

Perhaps the time had come for him to find a job and a place to live in town, he thought, as he watched Erin pedal her new pink tricycle up the sidewalk.

If Faith had been serious about moving here with their baby then he wanted to be near at hand in case they needed him.

Wade had expected Faith to see the sense of his marriage proposal. Her unexpected refusal had shocked him, but he understood why she had done it. He hadn't been able to tell her that he loved her.

She needed to be loved. She deserved to be loved. Just not by him.

The hell of it was, Wade couldn't get her out of

his head. He enjoyed being with her. He liked the way she had made him feel whole again. And the thought of another man loving her was intolerable. Somehow he would make her see that it made sense to marry him.

"Uncle Wade! Hurry up!" Erin interrupted his thoughts.

Wade focused on the task at hand, something he found himself repeating a thousand times a day since Faith had left.

Which meant that he thought about Faith a thousand times a day—or more, he thought ruefully.

"Here I come, Erin! Stop at the corner and turn around, okay?"

"Look! There's Mommy!" Erin hollered and waved at her mother and rang her tricycle bell as Sarah drove by with Ethan. Her short legs propelled the trike back toward the house as fast as they could.

Sarah pulled the car into the yard and climbed out, a wide smile on her face..

Erin pedaled into the drive screaming with glee with Wade at her side.

"Mommy! Mommy!"

Wade grinned at Sarah, opened the car's rear door and plucked Ethan from his car seat.

"So how's the little guy doing?" Wade asked as he tossed Ethan into the air above him. Ethan squealed with delight and Wade repeated the action. He couldn't wait to do this with his own child, he thought.

The intense desire to be a father constricted his chest, making it hard to breath. He handed Ethan over to Sarah and took the diaper and grocery bags from the back seat.

"Thanks. Somedays I wish I had been born an octopus. The doctor said Ethan's doing great, hitting all his percentile's. He's going to be as tall as you and Rafe, lucky guy. Thanks for watching Erin for me. It's been a treat having you here at the house, Wade. I actually get a little me time with you around."

Wade marveled at how fast Sarah could talk while multitasking, and all the while wearing a smile to boot. Rafe had been smart to marry the little blonde firecracker who had actively pursued him after high school. They made a good team.

He envied Rafe. Envied his cousin's warm and welcoming home and his family—both things Wade had always assumed he would have one day. Until Susan was murdered and his life imploded.

No, he corrected himself. He had assumed he would have a family until the day Susan told him she wanted a divorce.

"Earth to Wade? You with us?" Sarah took a grocery bag from Wade and set it on the counter, then slid the diaper bag from his shoulder.

Wade shook off his melancholia and forced a smile.

"I'm here. You're welcome, Sarah—I'm happy to help. I've enjoyed my stay here with the Winehurst clan. The kids are great. I was just thinking about how lucky Rafe is that he wised up and married you."

Sarah grinned, but before she could reply there was a knock on the door.

Mayhew entered the kitchen a moment later. He hugged Sarah and Erin and shook Ethan's chubby hand. The baby gurgled back at him.

"How is everyone?" asked Mayhew as he grabbed a chair from the table and straddled it.

Sarah told him about Ethan's physical and then excused herself to put the kids down for their naps.

Mayhew waited for Sarah to leave. "And how are you, cuz? I'm surprised to see you here. I didn't know you had left the cabin."

Wade shrugged. "I'm good." He didn't feel quite as comfortable around Mayhew as he felt with Rafe. Rafe was more like a brother, while Mayhew would always feel more distant, like a cousin.

Wade wondered why that was. The three cousins had grown up together but he and Rafe had always been closest, perhaps because they were the same age and Mayhew was two years older.

Or perhaps the separation grew because Mayhew's mother had run off with another man when Mayhew was ten and he had developed an unforgiving attitude toward women after that.

Mayhew dated, but never the same woman for more than a month or two. He always found something wrong with them to justify his dumping them.

Mayhew's brown eyes stared at Wade. He beetled his brows into a frown.

"Why are you here? Have you heard from Faith? I thought you were finished with her when I drove her back to Falmouth, but Susan told me you went down to see her last week. What gives?"

Mayhew lived in Portland where he held a job as an investment manager. He didn't know that Wade had asked Faith to marry him.

Wade briefly filled his cousin in on his trip to see Faith and her refusal to marry him. He didn't tell Mayhew about the baby.

His cousin's face flushed red and his scowl had deepened by the time Wade finished.

"That bitch. You asked her to marry you and she refused? You put yourself on the line for her and she turned you down?" Mayhew slammed a fist into his open palm.

"How could she turn you down?" he demanded. "That's not right, Wade. What are you going to do about it?"

Wade stood and placed his hand on Mayhew's arm. He didn't want to talk about Faith anymore, especially with Mayhew.

"It's okay, cuz," Wade said. "Faith and I will work something out, I'm sure. It's not as though I can force the woman to marry me." He smiled and changed the subject. Sometimes Mayhew could get a little too tightly wound when it came to women.

Sarah returned to the kitchen and the three caught up on recent news concerning other family members and friends. An hour later, Mayhew excused himself and left.

The house grew quiet once Mayhew had gone and with the children down for their naps. Sarah and Wade remained in the sunny kitchen and shared a lunch of thick ham and cheese sandwiches on homemade bread.

"This is one of my favorite times of the day," Sarah sighed. "I love my children, but I love my breaks from them as well. The only peace I get is when they're asleep, bless their little hearts."

She picked up their lunch plates and loaded them into the dishwasher, then leaned her back against the counter and crossed her arms over her chest.

"What are you going to do about Faith, Wade?"

Wade sat forward with his forearms resting on his knees and stared out the windows at the greening lawn.

"Mayhew asked me the same thing. I don't know, Sarah. I offered to marry her to be there for the baby and she said no. What more can I do?"

"Wade Elliot, do *not* tell me that you offered Faith marriage as a business proposition. Good grief. No wonder she turned you down. A woman needs to be loved, Wade. She needs to know she's wanted. How could you be so dumb? You're one of the most intelligent men I know."

Wade felt a flush creep up his neck.

"I loved Susan and it wasn't enough. She wanted a divorce, Sarah. A divorce! I wanted to start a family and she asked for a divorce." He looked at Sarah, his expression angry.

"The terrible thing, the thing that I can't forgive myself for, is that she wanted to move out and I talked her into staying another month. If I had only let her leave, Susan would still be alive today."

Sarah walked across the kitchen and pulled out the chair, placing it in front of Wade. She sat and placed her hands on on his knees and leaned forward until their faces were only inches apart.

"You listen to me, Wade Elliot. Faith is a very different woman from Susan. I don't think Susan ever truly loved you. She only married you to get out of Maine. She was bound to ask for a divorce sooner or later. When you told her you wanted to start a family she knew it was time to get out before she became tied down with a child."

Wade stiffened and narrowed his eyes at Sarah.

"I don't believe you. Susan could have left Greenville anytime. She didn't need to marry me."

Sarah squeezed his knees and leaned back, dropping her hands to her lap. Her expression was sympathetic when she continued.

"Think about it Wade. Susan never acted independently or did anything for herself. She used people to get what she needed. If you look at your marriage to her honestly I think you'll understand what I'm saying. Susan never loved you."

Wade started to defend Susan and Sarah lifted her palm before he could speak.

"Faith loves you. Her love for you shines in her eyes whenever she says your name. And judging by the way you've been mooning around here since she turned you down, I'd guess that you love her back. You're just too thick skulled to realize it. I love you like a brother Wade, so I have to tell you that you're acting like a pig headed fool."

Sarah stood and headed out of the kitchen.

"I'm going to take a nap while the munchkins are asleep. Leave me a note if you head back to Falmouth," she said over her shoulder.

Wade felt as if he'd been poleaxed. He stood and walked to the large doors and let himself out onto the deck. Ice was out on the southern tip of the huge lake and the deep blue water sparkled.

Could Sarah be right? Was it true that Susan

had never loved him? He thought back over his relationship with Susan, trying to view it objectively.

He and Susan had been high school sweethearts, but Wade had always assumed they would go their separate ways after school.

Susan had looked him up whenever he returned to Greenville during his college breaks, and he had fallen back into the relationship because Susan made it easy. He could see that now.

When the Boston Police offered Wade a job, Susan told him she was pregnant. Knowing how gossip spread in a small town, he had never told anyone about that. They had married and moved to Boston. Two months later Susan told him she miscarried the baby. By then he was too busy with the new job to question the miscarriage.

Now he wondered if Susan had truly been pregnant when they married. He had always used protection with her when they had sex. Maybe Sarah was right. Perhaps he and Susan had never truly loved one another. Perhaps they had never been more than good friends with a shared history.

He knew that Susan had never set him on fire the way that Faith did. He missed the feel of Faith's long, strong legs wrapped around him, and her beautiful eyes that turned more green than blue when she was turned on, staring up at him half-glazed with lust.

Wade's belly tightened.

He could no longer hide. He needed to face the truth. Was this burning need he felt for Faith love? Faith warmed the dark, cold space in his chest.

She made him feel interested in life again. She made him a better person. She made him feel human again.

He couldn't imagine living out the remainder of his years without her at his side to share them.

And that's when he knew.

He loved and needed Faith Donahue.

Wade grinned and let himself back inside the house. Damn that Sarah! How'd she get so smart anyway?

He found a piece of drawing paper and one of Erin's crayons and left Sarah a note. "Went to fetch me a wife, W."

He was whistling as he crossed the driveway and jumped into his rental SUV.

21

Faith hit the SEND button, shut down Safari, and closed her new laptop with a satisfied sigh. Yesterday her real estate agent had accepted an offer on the house for five thousand more than the list price. Faith had thirty days to find a rental and move out.

She had spent the morning looking online at houses for rent in Greenville, contacting the owners or agents handling the various properties by email. Hopefully one of them would pan out.

Three bedroom year round leases were scarce in a summer tourist town like Greenville. Landlords preferred to rent their properties to short term renters who were willing to fork out the higher summer rates for a two week vacation. Two bedroom homes were a little more common, but she needed the third bedroom for her writing office.

Faith's stomach growled, reminding her that it was well past lunch time. It seemed that she was always hungry these days. She wondered if that was what pregnant women meant when they talked about eating for two.

Not that she had talked with any other pregnant women. So far, all her knowledge came from the pregnancy books she had picked up from the Falmouth library. Only her doctor knew that Faith was pregnant.

And Wade. Wade knew. She still marveled over the way he had figured it out. He must have been a good detective before he went off the rails.

Faith pushed aside the thoughts of Wade and padded down the stairs to the kitchen. Knowing she needed to eat well for the baby, she had fully stocked the cupboards and fridge with her favorite foods.

For a while, eating had been a problem. Her stomach had been tied up in knots—first with the discovery that she was pregnant and the father didn't love her, then with confronting Hope and her destructive ways, and finally with her decision to turn down Wade's marriage proposal.

She still agonized over that last one.

Fortunately her healthy appetite had returned. Faith grabbed a loaf of sourdough bread from the bread box, sliced off two pieces, and set them on a small plate. The yeasty-sour smell of sourdough filled her nose.

Faith loved sourdough. It possessed an aroma that was different from any other bread, an aroma that made her picture old-fashioned kitchens with huge fireplaces and butcher block surfaces, copper and black iron pots and pans hanging from ceiling racks.

She pulled a jar of roasted red peppers and a wedge of cheddar cheese from the fridge, and grabbed her favorite knife, a steel Japanese-made paring knife that held an extra sharp edge.

After slicing thick chunks of the cheese, she added a drained pepper and several leafs of lettuce to the sandwich, then cut it into fourths. She had never been fond of halved sandwiches, preferring the smaller triangles her mother used to cut for her.

Faith ate two of the quarters and decided she needed a cup of tea. She knew she should be drinking milk for the extra calcium, but she hated milk. She made a mental note to look up other sources of calcium while she heated the tea water.

She was about to sit down with her tea mug when a knock came at the door.

"Shoot." Faith did not want to answer the door. She ran through the possibilities of who could be knocking at this time of day.

Not Hope. Faith hadn't heard from her sister since the day she'd told Hope not to come back. She would never let Hope into her home again and she felt at peace with that.

It wasn't the real estate agent. They had talked earlier this morning and everything was set until the home inspection next week.

It wouldn't be Mrs. Reynolds. Unless there was some sort of emergency.

Worried now, Faith set down her tea mug and headed for the front door. The knock repeated, louder and more insistent.

Definitely not Mrs. Reynolds. Her arthritic hands could never pound that loud.

She glanced out the sidelight and saw a black SUV parked in front of the house. Wade? What was he doing here?

Her heart leaped at the possibility of seeing Wade again. She smoothed her hair and wished she had dressed in something more attractive than old sweatpants and a faded men's shirt.

Could Wade be here to ask her to marry him again? Faith closed her eyes for a moment. She hoped so. This time she would say yes.

It didn't matter if Wade didn't love her, she loved him and wanted to be with him. She wanted to be a family: her, Wade, and Simon.

Smiling, Faith flung the door open. The smile

froze on her face when she saw Mayhew standing on the door stoop.

"Mayhew! What . . . what are you doing here?"

"May I come in, please?" Mayhew didn't wait for Faith to answer. He stepped forward, forcing her to retreat, and closed the door behind him.

Faith frowned at her visitor. "Has something happened to Wade?" she asked, suddenly fearful.

Mayhew turned to the door and threw the deadbolt.

"Yes, something's happened to Wade," he said.

Mayhew seemed to fill the narrow hallway. Faith retreated another step. Why had he locked her door?

Habit, she reassured herself. Mayhew lived in the city where most people kept their doors locked, even when home. He was simply being cautious.

"What's happened to Wade?" Faith lifted her hand to her chest. It suddenly felt tight and she was having trouble breathing. Images of Wade lying bleeding in the cabin with no one to help filled her mind.

"Tell me, please. Is he hurt? What's happened?"

Mayhew turned to face her. His fist struck her on the cheek, snapping her head back.

Faith stumbled backward into the wall. Her hand flew to her face. She stared at Mayhew through tear filled eyes, not quite believing that the man standing next to her had just hit her in the face.

Why had Mayhew hit her in the face?

"*You* happened, Faith," Mayhew said. "Wade was doing okay until you showed up and messed with him. I can't let you get away with that."

A small coil of fear began to unfurl deep in Faith's belly.

"I didn't—"

Mayhew's fist shot toward her again, catching her on the mouth this time.

Faith cried out and fell to the floor. She looked up into Mayhew's angry eyes and tried to think of how to make him understand. She tasted blood on her lips.

"Mayhew, I never—"

"SHUT UP! You're no better than that bitch Susan, but I set her straight. She learned not to mess with my cousin. Too bad she died, but I think it was for the best."

Mayhew reached down and pulled Faith to her feet by her shirt front. He hit her again, in the left temple this time.

Mayhew's fist caught her left eye next. Faith whimpered. Sparks of light danced in front of her face like mini-pinwheel fireworks.

She had seen the same display when Hope had hit her in the face with the wooden bat. Her face felt as if it were on fire. The coil of fear grew until it filled her entire body.

"Susan . . . what about Susan?" she asked through swollen lips.

"Susan never loved Wade. Wade gave her everything and she wanted to leave him. It's what women do. It's what you did. Wade suffered because of Susan and now he's suffering because of you, but he's too good to do anything about it. Lucky for him, I'm willing to settle the score."

Faith looked up at the crazy man holding her upright by her shirt and wondered what wires had twisted in Mayhew's brain. She had to make him understand that she loved Wade.

Understanding penetrated Faith's pain and fear.

"You . . . you killed Susan." Susan hadn't said "blame you" to Wade, she had tried to say "Mayhew."

Oh god. Mayhew was going to beat her to death, just like he had beaten Susan to death.

Faith's fear turned to terror. She was going to die and her baby was going to die with her. She couldn't let that happen. She had to protect her baby.

Faith kneed Mayhew. His grip loosened slightly, enough for her to jerk away. She ran toward the kitchen, looking for a way to get out of the house. The windows were no good; they were all modern, narrow crank-outs. She would never fit through them.

She kept the back door locked. It would take her precious moments to unlock it. Moments that would give Mayhew time to catch up with her, but it was the only other way out.

Behind her Mayhew roared her name and came after her, his boots thudding on the hall's wood floor.

Faith tried to scream, but Mayhew grabbed the back of her shirt and threw her against the kitchen door jamb. She fell into the kitchen, turned onto her stomach, and scrambled away from him.

"Bitch! You filthy bitch! You're all alike. You can't escape."

Mayhew picked Faith up and shook her until she feared her neck would snap, then threw her back to the floor. He kicked her in the shoulder, swearing at her and calling her ugly names.

Faith scrambled farther into the kitchen on her hands and knees. Her vision blurred.

She had to get to the back door. She had to get out of the house before she passed out.

She prayed that Mrs. Reynolds would somehow know something was wrong and call the police.

Mayhew kicked her in the ribs. She slammed against the kitchen table leg and tried to pull herself underneath.

She had to protect the baby. If Mayhew kicked

her in the abdomen he'd hurt the baby. She mustn't let him kick the baby. She had to stay alive for her baby. Wade's baby.

She had to protect Wade's baby.

"Whore! I'll teach you not to toy with my cousin."

Spittle flew from Mayhew's lips. His face was flushed deep red and covered in a thin sheen of sweat. His eyes were glazed with anger. A blue vein pulsed on the side of his forehead and disappeared under his blond bangs.

Mayhew grabbed Faith's left foot and dragged her to the center of the kitchen floor. He kicked her in the chest and back several times with the toe of his heavy boot before he lifted her to her feet again.

Faith was crying now. Great hiccuping sobs that made it hard to breathe and that hurt her bruised body. Her left eye had swollen shut and her mouth and head were bleeding.

Every sob jarred her chest and back with a pain so sharp it made her want to throw up.

Some remnant of her thinking brain told her that if she didn't find a way to defend herself in the next couple minutes she would soon be dead.

Mayhew's fist slammed into her ear.

Faith cried out and retched from the pain. How much more could she could endure before she fell unconscious?

Mayhew would kill her once she passed out.

A dizzy nausea filled her.

She had to stay on her feet. She fell against the counter and turned to grab it with both hands.

Don't fall. She mustn't fall again. He could kick her if she was on the floor. She had to stay off the floor.

Mayhew couldn't kick the baby if she stayed on her feet.

As she slumped against the counter, Faith's hands slid over the cutting board. The knife she had used on the cheese sat on the counter beside the board.

The blade was small but very, very sharp.

Faith gripped the knife handle tightly in her right hand and tried to shake off the darkness that pressed in on her and threatened her vision.

She knew she was only moments from eternal oblivion. Just like Susan. Only this time Wade wouldn't arrive in time to hear Faith accuse Mayhew of her own murder.

Unless she found a way to leave a mark on May-hew, no one would ever know who killed her. She had to leave an obvious mark.

Wade would figure it out if she could find a way to leave him a clue.

She accepted now that she was going to die. Mayhew was too big and strong for her to fight him off any longer. But perhaps she could leave

Wade a final gift, the gift of knowing that he wasn't responsible for Susan's death.

If she could hang on long enough to mark Mayhew's face with the knife, Wade would see the similarities between her and Susan's deaths and he would know. He would know because he had once been a good detective.

She took a last look out the kitchen window and silently apologized to her unborn son for not protecting him from the madman who was about to kill them both.

Mayhew grabbed Faith's left shoulder and spun her around. She whipped the knife around as she turned, aiming high.

She wanted to slash Mayhew's cheek and give him a long and deep cut that would require stitches and leave a scar, but she misjudged Mayhew's height and her own weakened state.

Instead of catching him on the cheek as she planned, Faith sliced into the side of his neck. Warm liquid sprayed over her face and down Mayhew's shirt.

His eyes widened and his hands flew to his neck.

Through blurry eyes Faith watched Mayhew's fingers turn red. *I'm hallucinating. I must be dying.*

She dropped the knife and took advantage of Mayhew's distraction to stumble away from him.

She made it two steps before crumpling to the kitchen floor.

She crawled on her hands and knees toward the back door. Every movement brought excruciating pain. Behind her she heard Mayhew hit the floor and knew he was after her again.

Darkness overtook her well before she reached the door.

Her last thoughts were of Wade and their baby. If she had only said yes when he offered to marry her, none of this would have happened.

Mayhew had been right.

This was all her fault.

22

———————

WADE PULLED into Faith's neighborhood and forced himself to keep to the posted speed limit. It wasn't easy. He couldn't wait to see her and hold her in his arms. Couldn't wait to see the look in her eyes when he told her that he loved her and asked her to marry him again.

This time she would say yes. He felt sure of it because she loved him too.

He pulled up behind a black SUV parked in front of Faith's house and turned off the engine. He frowned at the SUV as he climbed out of his rental. A quick glance at the quiet facade of Faith's house told him nothing.

Wade walked up to the driver's door and peered inside. He recognized the familiar Portland Pirate's ball cap sitting on the passenger seat. It was his cousin's current favorite. Why was Mayhew here?

Wade walked up the short walkway to the front door and knocked. He jingled the change in his pocket while he waited two full minutes, but heard no sounds from inside. Had Faith and Mayhew gone somewhere together on foot?

He knocked again and waited. An uneasiness came over him. He could think of no reason for Faith and Mayhew to go someplace together unless they had become friends.

That was a possibility, he conceded, as Mayhew lived nearby in downtown Portland. But if Mayhew and Faith had become friends, why hadn't his cousin mentioned it when Wade saw him at Sarah and Rafe's?

Wade cupped his hands and peered through the sidelight. The half-table Faith kept in the hall lay on its side. He frowned and crossed the front of the house, leaping over the waist high fence that blocked off the narrow side yard from the street.

He worked his way down the side of the house peering into the living room windows as he went but saw nothing else out of place.

"You there, what do you think you're doing? I'm calling the cops right now, young man. You have no business snooping on my neighbor."

Wade looked over his shoulder at the tiny, gray haired woman standing at the front corner of the next door house. She had one hand on top of a cane. The other held a cell phone.

"You don't have to worry, Mrs . . . ?"

"Reynolds. My name is Mrs. Reynolds. Faith and I look out for each other. Why are you sneaking down the side of her house?" Mrs. Reynolds glared at Wade.

"I was a detective with the Boston police department, ma'am. I saved Faith's life a couple months ago. Perhaps she mentioned me? My name is Wade. Wade Elliot."

The glare on Mrs. Reynolds's face grew more fierce. She pointed the cell phone at Wade.

"You're the idiot that doesn't recognize a good woman when he has one. Faith is special, Mr. Elliot, and you are a fool."

Wade couldn't help himself, he smiled at the old lady.

"Yes, ma'am, you got that right. I *was* a fool, but I'm here to make things right with Faith. I love her and I want to marry her."

Jesus it felt good to say that out loud. "Do you know where she is?"

Mrs. Reynolds narrowed her eyes at Wade. After a moment of silence she pointed at the house with her cane.

"She should be home. I saw a young man arrive about thirty minutes ago and they haven't left."

"They're not answering the door." Wade's brow

furrowed. What if Mayhew and Faith really had become friends?

Or worse, what if Mayhew had made a move on Faith and they were in bed together at this very moment? A fierce stab of jealousy knifed through him.

The neighbor waved toward the back of Faith's house. "Knock at the back door," she said. "They're likely in the kitchen and they didn't hear you."

His heart still pounding with jealous anger, Wade resumed walking down the side yard. Just shy of the back corner of the house, he looked up at a window over his head and saw streaks of red running down the glass.

He blinked and looked again. His heart stuttered and missed several beats before his years on the police force kicked in.

"Mrs. Reynolds! Call nine one one! Request an ambulance!" He shouted over his shoulder as he ran the last few feet and rounded the back corner of the house, leaping onto the top step in two long strides.

The back door was locked. Wade kicked at it. Once. Twice. Desperation gave him strength and on the third try the door sprang open.

Wade rushed through the door and stopped cold. He stared at the scene before him with his heart in his mouth and ice in his veins.

There was blood everywhere. His cousin

Mayhew lay in a large puddle of red, an ugly, open gash visible on the side of his neck, his shirt front soaked with blood, his eyes open and sightless.

Blood spatters covered the kitchen walls, floor, and countertops.

Faith's kitchen looked and smelled like a slaughterhouse.

Faith lay on her side, halfway between Mayhew and the rear door, one arm outstretched, as if she had been reaching for something, the other curled around her belly.

In the distance, sirens wailed.

Wade knew that it was wrong to enter a crime scene before the local police arrived, but he had to know if Faith still lived.

He stepped directly to Faith and knelt beside her. He turned her over gently and couldn't bite back his cry of pain when he saw her swollen and bloody face. What had happened here?

Like Mayhew, Faith lay in a pool of blood, already sticky and drying. Was it her blood or his cousin's?

He smoothed the stiff, blood-encrusted hair away from Faith's neck and felt for a pulse. For several long moments he felt nothing and a despair worse than the one that had destroyed him five years earlier took hold.

"Faith. Don't leave me," he whispered. "I need

you. You have to live, dammit. You hear me? I need you. I love you."

A feeble pulse throbbed beneath his fingers and tears began to leak from Wade's eyes.

"Yes, darling," he encouraged. "Live for me. I don't know what I'd do if I lost you."

He sat beside Faith, found her hand, and laced his fingers through hers. He yearned to gather her in his arms, but didn't dare lift her, afraid that if he moved her he would make her injuries worse.

While Wade waited for the ambulance to arrive he prayed to any higher power that happened to be listening not to take this beautiful woman from him just when he had realized how much he needed her.

The ambulance and the police arrived at the same time. Wade identified himself, told the police what he knew, and accompanied Faith to the hospital in the ambulance.

The next eight hours seemed to last a lifetime. Two Portland detectives came to the hospital and questioned him extensively. He understood why they had to do it. They had found him on the scene of a murder and brutal beating. For all they knew he had done it.

Fortunately Mrs. Reynolds showed up and told the detectives that he had only just arrived at Faith's house and found Mayhew and Faith, sparing him a trip to police headquarters.

He filled out the required paperwork for Faith, putting himself down as next of kin. Although he eventually sent her neighbor home in a cab, Wade refused to leave the hospital while he waited for Faith to come out of surgery for a ruptured spleen.

He thought his heart would break when the surgeon told him that Faith had miscarried their baby. He knew then that the miscarriage had most likely been the source of the blood beneath Faith.

Her doctor assured Wade that despite Faith's extensive injuries there had been no permanent damage to her womb. She would be able to bear children again after she healed from Mayhew's beating.

Wade nodded impatiently while the doctor talked, his mind focused only on the woman lying in recovery. He didn't care if he couldn't have children with Faith.

The important thing was that he had Faith. They could always adopt a family.

Faith opened her right eye and closed it against the bright light. Where was she? Every part of her face and body ached and hurt. Her abdomen hurt especially bad.

"Has she been awake yet?"

Faith heard the whisper. She recognized Mrs.

Reynold's scratchy voice and tried to smile. The movement hurt her lips and cheeks and brought back her memory.

Mayhew. Mayhew had tried to kill her, but apparently she hadn't died.

She focused on the sounds and smells around her. Something beeped at regular intervals near her head. She smelled iodine and disinfectant and roses. Roses?

Faith realized she was in the hospital. That couldn't be a good thing. She hoped the hospital personnel were smart enough not to let Mayhew get near her.

She needed to warn them.

She jerked her arm and immediately felt a large, warm hand grasp her own and stroke the back of it.

"Shhh, sweetheart, it's okay. You're going to be fine."

She'd know Wade's smooth, deep voice anywhere. What was Wade doing with her in the hospital?

Faith opened her eye again and looked into a pair of concerned deep blue eyes. Wade's eyes. She drank in every detail of his face, the face of the man she loved.

He looked as if he hadn't slept or shaved in several days. He looked so beautiful. Her lips parted.

"I . . ." Her face hurt too much to talk.

"Shhhh. Don't talk. Mayhew put a serious hurt on you. It will take a few days for the swelling to go down. Go back to sleep. I'm going to be right here when you wake up. I'm never letting you out of my sight again."

Faith slid back into unconsciousness. She trusted Wade. He would watch over her and protect her from Mayhew. When she could talk she would tell him about Mayhew and Susan.

~

"Hello, dearie. It's nice to see you with us again." Mrs. Reynolds smiled at Faith.

"Wade?" Had he left her already? Her heart ached from the hurt. Of course he had. Wade didn't love her.

"I made him go down to the cafeteria for some breakfast. He hasn't left your side since you were admitted two days ago. The poor man is wasting away. You've landed yourself a good one there, Faith. If I was younger I'd give you some competition. That man is s-e-x-y sexy. He even gets my ancient motor running." Mrs. Reynolds cackled and smiled at Faith.

Faith gave a lop-sided smile back. Her face didn't feel as swollen, but her abdomen was still tender and it hurt to breath.

The baby! Panic washed through her. She grabbed at the bed sheets.

"My baby. How is my baby?"

Mrs. Reynolds patted Faith's hand.

"I'll let your young man tell you about everything. Oh good, here he is now." Mrs. Reynolds gave up her seat beside the bed.

"She wants to know about the baby," she said in a loud whisper to Wade on her way out.

Mrs. Reynolds turned back to Faith with a sympathetic expression.

"I'll see you tomorrow, dearie. You keep resting so you can get out of here and come home."

Did Mrs. Reynolds think that Faith couldn't hear her? Fear gripped Faith. Why wouldn't she tell her about the baby?

"What happened to my baby? Wade, tell me."

Wade took the vacated seat and gently grasped Faith's hand between both of his own.

"You miscarried the baby, sweetheart. There was too much trauma to your body. Mayhew ruptured your spleen and broke four ribs."

He had to stop speaking for a moment and wait for the rage that engulfed him to ebb.

"The surgeon said the miscarriage was for the best," he continued. "The baby had most likely been damaged. The good news is there was no permanent damage to your body and you'll be able to have more children. I'm sorry, sweetheart. I'm so, so sorry."

Tears flowed down Faith's cheeks. She had tried so hard to protect her baby from Mayhew's beating, but she had failed. She had failed her son.

"Mayhew killed my baby." Faith gave Wade a fierce glare with her good eye. "He'd better be in jail. He has to pay for what he did," she said. "He killed Susan too. He told me."

Wade rubbed the back of her hand with his thumb. He stared into Faith's right eye. The left one was still mostly swollen closed. He tried not to let the shock of seeing her battered and bruised show on his own face.

He'd been staring at Faith for the last forty-eight hours and he still felt horrified by what his cousin had done to her. He took a deep breath and let it out.

"Mayhew is dead, Faith. He'll never hurt anyone again."

"What?" Panic gripped Faith. She struggled to sit up but dropped back at the stabbing pain in her chest.

"Oh no, Wade. You didn't kill him, did you? I don't want you to go to jail."

Wade hesitated. He didn't know if he should tell Faith that when she cut Mayhew's neck she hit his carotid artery and his cousin had bled out before Wade had arrived at her house.

The police had concluded that Faith had killed Mayhew in self-defense. Did she need to hear that on top of the news about the miscarriage?

No, he decided. That could wait until she felt stronger.

"No, sweetheart, I didn't kill him. Go back to sleep. We'll talk more later."

Wade watched Faith close her eye. He still couldn't believe that Mayhew had meant to kill Faith and that he had also killed Susan.

He regretted his cousin's death but he was thankful that Faith had survived and not Mayhew.

The hard truth was that if he had arrived while Mayhew was beating the woman he loved he might have killed his cousin himself.

No, he amended silently, looking at Faith's battered body. He *would* have killed Mayhew.

It would take time for Faith to deal with losing the baby and Mayhew's assault and death, but Wade would help her through the nightmares that were bound to come. He wasn't letting Faith out of his sight again.

At least not until they were married.

EPILOGUE

Five Years Later

"Simon, give Mark back his shovel." Faith bent down awkwardly and handed the dark-haired boy the shovel he had tossed aside in favor of his twin's.

"Oof." She stood and waddled to a lawn chair and sat next to Sarah. Both women were eight months pregnant; Sarah with her fourth child (she swore it would be her last), and Faith with her third.

Faith looked out over the sunlit bog and sighed with contentment. She loved visiting the cabin any time of the year, but especially in the fall. The bright, vibrant colors surrounding the golden tannin-stained water and the deep blue of the sky were too beautiful for words.

A late dragonfly darted over the cattails that grew at the right hand edge of the slope, his translucent wings iridescent in the sun's rays.

Crows cawed in the distance. A vee of geese flying south passed overhead, calling to one another. Faith breathed the scent of balsam and pine deep into her lungs.

The cabin represented peace and a new beginning for Faith. She had recovered from Mayhew's attack here with Wade's help, and now their children played here with their cousins the same way Wade and Rafe and Mayhew had played here as youngsters.

Rafe and Sarah had felt close to Mayhew and had a difficult time accepting that Mayhew had been responsible for Susan's murder.

They blamed themselves for not realizing how deep his distrust and hatred of women had been. If they had realized, they might have been able to get psychiatric help for Mayhew before anyone had been hurt hurt.

While Faith would never forgive Mayhew for the loss of her first baby she also felt compassion for the unloved little boy he had once been.

Months of therapy following Mayhew's attack had helped her to accept the fact that she hadn't meant to kill Mayhew, she had only done what any mother would do to protect her unborn child.

It had taken more than a year for the nightmares and depression to pass. Faith had cried long and hard when she learned that the baby she had lost had indeed been a boy.

She and Wade had held a small, private service for him and planted a willow tree beside the bog in his memory. The willow had already tripled in size and gave Faith comfort whenever she looked at it.

When she learned she was pregnant again with the twins she had insisted that they plant another willow in Mayhew's memory.

It stood on the opposite side of the slope from the first willow, bracketing the cabin's view of the bog.

The twin boys, Mark and Simon, had been a handful as infants. At the age of three they were downright precocious.

Faith observed them with a proud grin. She wouldn't have it any other way. They were just like their father. Dark haired, blue eyed, and full of mischief.

Wade sauntered over to the women and sat on the ground beside Faith. He placed a hand on her swollen belly and leaned over to kiss it.

When he lifted his head his look gave Faith a thrill. There was no mistaking the love and heat in his eyes.

Wade had turned out be everything she could ever have hoped for in a husband and lover and an inspiration for her writing. She smiled back at him with a promise in her eyes.

The two male cousins were building an addition onto the cabin, a bunk room large enough to hold the newest generation of cousins and the adults when they visited.

It was the first of two that were planned. Next year they'd add a second wing to the opposite side of the cabin so each family would have their own sleeping/private space.

Wade and Faith had lived in the cabin until the twins were born. They had eventually moved to Greenville to be close to schools and Rafe's family, but they returned to the place where they had first met and fell in love at every opportunity.

"Are you ladies enjoying watching us men work?" Wade asked in a teasing tone.

"It's only fair," Faith said with an answering smile, "since you and the boys watch me work all the time."

Faith placed her hand on her round belly. "I sure hope this one is a girl. I like you boys well enough, but I need a little girl so I don't feel quite so outnumbered."

Wade's mouth curved into the sexy grin that made her body feel weak and her heart do flip-flops.

"Well, if it's not, we'll just keep trying until we get it right," he promised.

Faith laughed. "That's what I love about you. You're a can-do sort of guy."

It had taken eighteen months for her to begin writing again. Her romances and newest mystery series had been well received by her fans. She was happily at work on her next effort.

After talking with a local art dealer, Wade had his collection of carvings reproduced in bronze and sold the bronzes through a Portland art gallery. Word of his work had spread and recently a gallery in New York City had also picked up his bronzes to sell.

"Unfair." Rafe plopped down on the ground beside Sarah after kissing the top of her head.

"Why am I working all alone while you get to sit with two beautiful women?"

"Obviously I'm way smarter than you, cuz." Wade winked at his wife.

Faith took a deep, satisfied breath and let it out. She felt happy, happier than she ever believed possible. She was surrounded by family. A real family. A loving family.

Family the way family was meant to be. Family that laughed together and supported one another and loved without reservation.

Wade had paid Hope a visit soon after Faith had been released from the hospital. He had told Hope that if she ever dared to show her face at their door he would have her arrested for attempting to murder Faith.

When he finally told Faith about his visit to her sister, Faith had asked how Hope had taken his warning. Wade had only taken her in his arms and kissed her silly instead of answering the question.

She didn't press him. She already knew that Hope would have been crazy with anger and jealousy when she learned that Faith had a strong, handsome man looking out for her.

Faith smiled. Maybe she should send Hope a thank you note.

Because of her twisted sister Faith had met the man of her dreams, a romantic hero worthy of his own romance novel.

Because of Hope she had become part of a family, a family to love and cherish and grow old with.

Because of Hope she was truly happy, and she knew that her happiness was the sweetest revenge against everything her sister had ever done to hurt her.

Faith's smile grew.

She really needed to send that note.

I'm glad you found this book out of the millions available. If you'd like to know when I release a new book instead of leaving it to chance you can sign up for my newsletter. You can also see what I'm working on or even send me an email– all through my website, CharleyMarshBooks.com

Turn the page for a preview of Artemis, the third book in the Romancing a God series.

ARTEMIS

TIA SMITH STRODE through the double etched-glass doors of Orion Development and scowled. Her first visit to the company her father had insisted she work with on the bayside project and she already hated them. In her opinion, a company who paid to have the constellation Orion etched into dark smoked glass along with their name in fancy script was a company who overcharged their clients.

Tia was fiercely protective of the people affected by her projects, and Bayside Commons was the largest project her young company had put together to date. The scope of the project would provide lots of opportunity for unscrupulous firms to pad costs and skim off the extra.

She was determined not to let that happen with

Bayside. She'd worked too hard setting the project up to let some arrogant businessman scupper it for her.

She paused just inside the glass doors and eyed the large, luxurious reception area. A half dozen brown leather club chairs ranged in cozy seating groups against one wood paneled wall to her right. Real wood paneling, she noted. Not that fake veneer crap that was all the rage in the last century.

The chairs were fronted by several glass coffee tables and faced a wall of windows looking out over Portland's harbor and working waterfront.

She smelled coffee, rich leather, and the faint briny smell of sea water that told her Orion Development believed in open windows.

Oil and watercolor paintings of Portland's early days hung on the paneled walls. A quick glance at the one closest to her told Tia they were originals by some of the city's finest artists.

The room looked like it belonged in a high class private men's club, not an office complex. It was an in your face reminder that Orion Development was so successful they could afford to waste a windowed wall, usually reserved for high-powered executives, on their waiting room, and consequently on their clients.

It was brilliant marketing.

Tia's scowled deepened. She despised ostentatiousness in any form. In her mind, Jack Orion's company displayed it in spades. She expected the man himself to be even worse. Damn her father and his meddling.

A little research into the highly public Orion had turned up a man who played hard and went through beautiful women like they were a bottomless commodity. In his life they probably were, she thought with disgust. Orion had everything shallow, status seeking babes wanted—money, prestige and power, and looks.

She headed across the lush deep blue carpet to the only person in the room. A receptionist sat erect behind a sleek desk built from polished mahogany that held a state of the art communication system and computer. A small name plaque identified her as Ashley Hayes.

Ms. Hayes matched the room—deep blue skirt suit, red-brown hair pulled back into a snug bun, everything neat and prim and well put together, make-up expertly applied to her slightly slanted eyes and generous lips.

In contrast, Tia was dressed to visit the building site in slim jeans, a faded Rolling Stones tee-shirt, and scuffed leather boots.

The receptionist stopped tapping the keyboard with her long nails and the faint clatter that Tia had detected upon entering the Orion offices stopped.

Much to her mother's dismay, Tia kept her own

nails neatly trimmed. She couldn't stand that tap-tap-tap that long nails made when working a keyboard, something she spent many hours at. That, plus the fact that Tia worked with her hands and often beat them up, meant short nails, no polish.

"Darling, how do you expect to attract a man when you don't make the most of your feminine qualities?" Her mother's voice echoed in Tia's head.

How many times had Tia listened to her mother's lectures on luring a man?

What her poor, well-meaning mother didn't understand was that Tia had her work. The job kept her busy, usually seven days a week. So far she hadn't met any men who were more interesting than her job.

The receptionist smiled with her deep red lips—lips that exactly matched her nails—a smile that did not reach her dark brown eyes. Tia wondered if the woman always coordinated her lips and nails. Why would a person do that? Didn't the woman have better things to do with her time?

"Welcome to Orion Development. How may I help you?"

The woman's voice was smooth and cool. Obviously she didn't understand the meaning of the word "welcome" as there was none in her tone.

"Tia Smith. I have an appointment with Jack Orion," Tia answered.

The receptionist clicked a few keys. "I see you

are scheduled to meet with Mr. Orion at ten o'clock."

"I just said that, didn't I? Let him know I'm here, please."

The receptionist's eyes grew even frostier. She turned away from Tia and tapped her headset. She spoke softly into it, then turned back to Tia.

"Mr. Orion will see you now," she said curtly as she rose from her desk. Even in sky high heels she barely came to Tia's shoulder. Wordlessly she walked to the back wall and opened a cleverly camouflaged door. She stepped into the office ahead of Tia.

Jack Orion's office had polished oak floors mostly covered by a large, blue Persian rug. The rug was old, the blue color far rarer than the more common red rugs. Tia's practiced eye could see that it had been well made, likely with several hundred knots per inch.

Floor to ceiling windows filled the wall to Tia's left with a leather sofa and two facing leather chairs attractively arranged in front of it. Shelves filled with books and models of buildings and ships lined the opposite wall. She had to admit that she liked the room, despite the fact that she was prepared not to like the room's occupant.

Tia's gaze rested on Jack Orion, seated behind a modern, black, U-shaped console holding three computers. He had yet to look up from the screen he was watching. "I'll be with you in a sec."

His voice was deep and smooth and softer than Tia had expected. She wondered if he sang. He had a great voice for it.

"Mr. Orion, Ms. Smith to see you." The receptionist hesitated, stepped closer to the desk. Her voice softened. "Can I get you anything, Jack? Coffee?" she asked.

"Not at the moment, Ashley. I'll let you know."

Tia watched them with detached curiosity. She found that observing the dynamics between people proved useful in her business dealings. The way a boss treated an employee told her a lot about the boss. Was he courteous? Patient? Or rude and demanding? Was the employee respectful? Over-familiar? Cowed?

It was obvious to Tia that the receptionist was definitely sweet on Jack Orion, but he had barely looked at her. He either didn't want to show any hint of romance in front of a stranger or he wasn't interested in Ashley.

The receptionist gave Tia another cold look and left the office, leaving the door open, most likely so she could eavesdrop on Tia's meeting with her boss.

Tia stepped over and closed the office door firmly behind Ashley, then moved to stand in front of the desk. This was a private meeting. She had a few things to set straight with Jack Orion and she didn't want any interruptions.

The man in question rose from his desk as she crossed the room. He was tall, at least six-five, with broad shoulders that filled out his perfectly-fitted suit, a handsome face framed by dark blonde hair in need of a cut. In short, he was cut from the same god-like cloth as Tia's brothers. Too damn attractive for their own good.

Jack Orion held out his hand. Warm and dry and powerful, it nearly engulfed Tia's own.

"It's good to finally meet you, Ms. Smith. I find it hard to take the measure of a man—or woman—through email or over the phone. I prefer personal meetings myself."

Dark blue eyes studied her intently. Tia could see faint lines radiating from their outer corners—whether from laughter or sun exposure she couldn't say.

"Why don't we move over to the windows while we talk?" he asked. "I find the activity on the docks fascinating."

He still held her hand. She gently freed herself. "Whatever you'd like, Mr. Orion," she said, cool and polite.

She had read everything she could find on Jack Orion and his company before making this appointment. Nothing she'd seen so far contradicted her findings. Handsome, athletic, and very wealthy—in essence Orion was a man used to having things his way.

The society reporters loved him. He often graced their pages with a different—always beautiful—woman at his side, attending the orchestra, museums, gallery openings, regattas. One of Portland's most eligible bachelors, Jack Orion was a big fish in the city of Portland.

She followed him to the seating area and took one of the chairs. Crossing her long legs she waited to see how he intended to address her concerns. He surprised her when he didn't dive immediately into business.

"I often nap on this couch," he said as he settled onto it. "But please don't tell my receptionist. Ashely believes I'm in here working my fingers to the bone when I tell her to hold all calls. I'd hate to have her image of me ruined." His blue eyes twinkled, inviting Tia in on his little secret.

Damn if she didn't want to smile at him. She pressed her lips together and reminded herself why she had made the trip across town to his office.

"Mr. Orion—" she began.

"Jack, please. We'll be working closely together for the next three years. Mr. Orion will be tedious to say and to hear after one week. May I call you Tia? That's what your friends call you, isn't it?"

Tia frowned. Her first meeting with Jack Orion was not going as planned. He kept derailing her.

"Call me whatever you like, Mr. Orion. "There are several points I want to clear up before we actually begin working together. I don't know how much my father told you about the Bayside Project–"

"Enough to get me interested." What her father hadn't told him was how beautiful his daughter was.

"That's what I'm afraid of. He probably told you about the office buildings and condominiums and neglected to tell you about–"

"Excuse me a moment, Tia. I think I'd like some coffee after all. Can I have Ashley bring a pot and two cups?"

Tia took a deep breath and reined in her temper. "Thank you, that would be nice." She smiled sweetly. If any of her brothers had seen that smile they'd know to run and run fast.

Five minutes later she sat with a cup of coffee balanced on her leg. She took a sip of the dark roasted brew and waited to see if the man across from her was going to come up with anything else to keep her from saying what she came to say.

Jack drank his coffee while he studied Tia Smith. She was not at all what he had expected. He was used to beautiful women. They flocked to him and enjoyed his companionship. He could easily place them all in a mold–beautiful features, perfect form, lovely clothes and jewels, soft and feminine.

The ones he dated more than once also possessed intelligence.

He had been surprised and intrigued when he shook Tia's hand to feel callouses on her palm. Most women who looked like Tia and had the money to do whatever they wanted had soft, weak hands. Hers had felt strong and firm. The hands of someone who actually did physical labor.

He found that strangely appealing.

Her physical presence filled his office. She had to stand nearly six foot in bare feet, with a lean, athletic body and a beautiful face framed by dark–nearly black–curls. Intelligence gleamed from her moss green eyes.

Those large eyes studied him now. He set down his coffee cup and leaned back on the sofa, put his feet up on the coffee table and prepared to spar with the lovely Tia. Anticipation made his blood quicken.

"So, you have a few points you wish to clear up before we move forward."

"Yes. I do, as a matter of fact. Did my father also tell you what I have planned to help with the housing shortage for the underprivileged?"

"He may have mentioned something about that being part of the project. We didn't get into details. He wanted to leave that up to you."

Tia stopped herself from rolling her eyes. Her father had a tendency to drop his children "in the soup" as they liked to say. He found it amusing to set them up in difficult situations so he could see how they wriggled out of them.

His children, on the other hand, were seldom amused by Father's little "lessons" as he called them.

"Oh, I think you must know more about my housing plan than you're admitting, Mr. Orion," Tia said mildly. "After all, didn't you leave a threatening letter and a cooler full of rotting fish heads on my doorstep?"

❧

You can find Artemis in digital, print, or Large Print at all your favorite retailers.

ABOUT THE AUTHOR

Charley Marsh's curiosity drove her to climb mountains, canoe rivers, and explore caves and wilderness areas from Maine to California. She's been shot at, caught in a desert flash flood, and almost drowned off the Maine coast. Once she tobogganed down a 5,000+ foot mountain.

Life is always an adventure if you have the right attitude.

Charley never set out to be a storyteller, but looking back on the elaborate lies she made up as a troubled teen she can see that she always had the makings. Now, in the immortal words of Lawrence Block, she happily "makes up lies for fun and profit."

If you would like information regarding Charley's latest releases or simply want to contact Charley visit:
https://charleymarshbooks.com/

www.ingramcontent.com/pod-product-compliance
Lightning Source LLC
Chambersburg PA
CBHW071235190726
48292CB00007B/2292